A Touch of Ruckus

ASH VAN OTTERLOO

Also by Ash Van Otterloo

Cattywampus

A
Touch of
Ruckus

ASH VAN OTTERLOO

SCHOLASTIC PRESS / NEW YORK

Library of Congress Cataloging-in-Publication Data

Names: Van Otterloo, Ash, author.
Title: A touch of ruckus / Ash Van Otterloo.
Description: New York: Scholastic Inc., 2021. | Audience: Ages 8–12. | Audience: Grades 4–6. | Summary: Twelve-year-old Tennessee Lancaster, burdened by her ability to pry into folks' memories by touching their belongings and by her prideful family's secrets, finds solace in ghost hunting with her nonbinary crush inside a nearby forest in Howler's Hollow, but when the ghosts reveal that the forest's existence is threatened, Tennie must find the link between how they died and her own family's secrets.
Identifiers: LCCN 2021003669 (print) | LCCN 2021003670 (ebook) | ISBN 9781338702033 (hardcover) | ISBN 9781338702040 (ebk)
Subjects: LCSH: Paranormal fiction. | Ghost stories. | Imaginary places—Juvenile fiction. | Secrecy—Juvenile fiction. | Friendship—Juvenile fiction. | Grandmothers—Juvenile fiction. | Families—Juvenile fiction. | CYAC: Parapsychology—Fiction. | Ghosts— Fiction. | Forests and forestry—Fiction. | Secrets—Fiction. | Friendship—Fiction. | Grandmothers—Fiction. | Families—Fiction. | LCGFT: Paranormal fiction.
Classification: LCC PZ7.1.V38 To 2021 (print) | LCC PZ7.1.V38 (ebook) | DDC 813.6 [Fic]—dc23
LC record available at https://lccn.loc.gov/2021003669
LC ebook record available at https://lccn.loc.gov/2021003670

1 2021

Printed in the U.S.A.   23
First printing, September 2021
Book design by Baily Crawford

TO THOSE WHO TAKE
THE BACK SEAT TO KEEP THE
PEACE: MAY YOU HAVE
BEAUTIFUL ADVENTURES,
ENJOY LOVE, AND KNOW
HOW ASTONISHING YOU ARE.

CHAPTER 1

Every time Tennessee Lancaster visited the Hollow, it got harder to tell where she stopped and where the forest began. Mist swirled across the back roads, dancing wild outside her half-lowered van window. Tennie's stomach did odd little cartwheels, as if the rippling fog squirmed inside her, too.

She jutted her chin closer to the opening. Damp air rushed over her freckled skin until her nose went numb. Autumn—Halloween especially—was her favorite time of year. She was determined to enjoy it properly, even if her family was moving. But as the trees whizzed by in an orange-and-ruby fury, Tennie's nerves couldn't settle.

Her family's new apartment—the one they'd just left all their moving boxes in—was a two-bedroom rental too small for all six of them. So they were making a pit stop at her grandmother's town an hour away. Her older brother, Birch, would stay with Mimsy for a month, while the rest of them crammed in like sardines.

"When we get there, I'll do the talking," Mama barked from the front seat, as "Monster Mash" blared on the radio. Her hyper fingers strummed the steering wheel. "Mimsy don't need to know about the housing mix-up."

Tennie didn't point out they'd all already been over this a dozen times. "Yes, ma'am."

"So here's the plan. Last week, she asked me to come help clean out Poppy's old things, which I'm not going to do. That woman can't ever stop complaining about my daddy, even now that he's passed. But Birch can go instead, as a favor to her. Problem solved."

Sadness at the thought of Poppy's things getting thrown out gripped Tennie, followed by a pang of jealousy. She'd have loved to be the one staying over at Mimsy's.

"Not as a favor to *us*?" Dad joked in a road-ragged voice from the passenger's seat. "If she says no, we're up a creek without a paddle here."

"Absolutely *NOT*. I won't have my mother fixin' my life like one of her dusty antiques," Mama muttered. "I'd never hear the end of it."

Tennie's legs clenched. She hated this ongoing pride war between Mama and Mimsy. "You know Mimsy loves us, Mama! And she always brags on what a good paramedic you are."

"That won't stop her from being proud as peas if she thinks she's saving Birch from sleeping on a couch. So stick to the story, got it? *Birch, d'you hear me?*"

THWUNK. Tennie's eyes narrowed when Birch's unnaturally long, cave-cricket legs knocked the back of her seat for the hundredth time as he shifted in his sleep. He wasn't even *listening.*

"We hear you, Mama—" Tennie said, covering for her brother. Her mom's shoulders loosened, and Tennie congratulated herself. She was the family's parent-whisperer. Once Birch was dropped off, and Mimsy was good and hoodwinked into thinking the Lancaster finances were fine, everyone's feathers would unruffle. Then, Tennie could relax, too, and enjoy her spooky fall season properly, with *Corpse Bride* marathons and candy corn.

But as Tennie imagined Birch lounging around Mimsy's

picture-perfect front porch, the restlessness in her gut grew wilder. Why did Captain Earbuds get rewarded for being a lazy pain, while Tennie worked hard to help everyone get along?

So, ask Mama and Dad if you can go instead, a rebellious flicker suggested for the hundredth time. *That way, you get a whole room to yourself. Finally.*

Tennie's fingers tensed in her rainbow-striped gloves, curling up like threatened spiders. The thought of opening her mouth to ask Mama to change her plans was unthinkable. Especially while Mama was this keyed up. "I can't be selfish," she whispered, fogging the glass by her nose.

Five-year-old Shiloh, the drooling mirror image of her sleeping twin, Harper, snuggled her head into Tennie's side, hugging her clown-faced Raggedy Andy doll—an antique Mimsy had gifted her, and who precocious Shi had renamed "Mr. Fancy Pants." Tennie sagged and smooched the top of her sister's sweaty auburn head. Both twins' French braids fuzzed out like halos, making them look more angelic than they were. *If I go to Mimsy's, these little monsters'll wear Mama slap out. Birch won't help, and she'll start getting blue again*, Tennie worried.

But the fire in her stomach wouldn't quiet. *Think of Mimsy's fireplace! A soft, giant bed, all to yourself! Hot breakfast every day!* The flames crackled. Tennie pressed her lips. Time to give it an ice-cold drenching. She peeled her left glove from her hand, slipping her bare fingers into her hoodie pocket. She grazed them across a shard of plastic she kept there.

Tennie inhaled sharply. Her own magic always unsettled her.

The van around her dissolved into smeary smoke, and a blurred memory from five years ago replaced it.

Her old living room fluttered with orange streamers and homemade ISN'T IT GREAT? TENNESSEE'S EIGHT! banners. Memory-Tennie twirled and walked tiptoe in a ruffled pumpkin-print dress. She pestered Mama, who balanced a cake on one arm and crying baby Shiloh in the other.

"Stop grabbing, Tennie!" Mama snapped. The scent of apple shampoo from her still-dripping shower hair tickled Tennie's nose. "Guests will be here any minute, and the kitchen still isn't clean! And you know how sanctimonious Mimsy gets about that!"

Birch trotted into the room holding a jar of spiders, then wrinkled his nose. "Ugh, what smells like toilets?"

Tennie gasped. She pointed at baby Harper in her playpen, who had just strewn the contents of her diaper in unthinkable places. "Ewwwww!"

"Gross!" Birch hollered, dropping his spider jar and

yarfing onto the floor. Tiny spiders fanned out from the broken glass in a skittering shadow, sending chills up Tennie's neck. She shrieked. Dad rushed in with paper towels as Mama tried to stamp the spiderlings with squeaking sneakers.

The doorbell rang. Mimsy let herself in and started fussing hard over the mess. Mama yelled that she didn't need Mimsy's help. A sour feeling filled Tennie's mouth at the sound of their arguing.

Everything was wrong. Fury rose in Tennie. Her family had ruined her birthday party before it began! Tennie hollered then, too. She yelled ugly, hateful words at her whole awful family. She snatched the party tiara from her head and snapped it into bits. Mama's face crumpled. She cried in the bedroom for hours, and Tennie cried in hers. Dad turned guests away, making up a story about a stomach bug. Mimsy cleaned the living room, then left, never bringing it up again.

Tennie yanked her trembling fingers from the shattered plastic. Her vision spun like a ceiling fan until the van grew solid around her. She pulled deep breaths through her nostrils and fixed a chill expression on her face, just in case her parents glanced in the rearview. The memory slowly fell asleep again, but the guilty feeling stayed in Tennie's gut, like the sore spot you got on your arm after a booster shot.

It worked like a charm. Tennie's anger fizzled. But that was no surprise. She'd smothered it this way a hundred times, and she had to admit, she felt a little smug over how good she'd gotten at it.

The first time she'd discovered her ability, it had been by accident. She'd clutched her shattered birthday tiara and forced herself to picture Mama's tears as her guilt coiled around her like a hungry snake. The memory had grown more and more real, until suddenly Tennie wasn't just *remembering* her crappy party—she was *at* her crappy party. Presently, Tennie's heart rate slowed. *Eighty beats per minute.* By now, she'd probably relived this particular scene hundreds of times, and she recovered from it faster than when she woke a brand-new memory.

Reliving the party was her anchor when her feelings got out of control—helping her keep her promise to herself to never add fuel to her family's problems again. Over time she'd discovered her ability was good for digging through other folks' memories, too. When they really cared about something, their recollections would get nice and stuck in an object, and Tennie was free to take it all in. Sometimes she just caught a feeling, and other times she practically time-traveled into the past.

But stealing memories could be upsetting. Sometimes, she hated what she found. Hidden sadness, secret worry, and real pain were more common than folks let on, making her super-power feel more like a superburden. But that's what the gloves were for. They kept the memories out.

Everybody's hiding something, Tennie thought, eyeballing the back of her parents' heads as the van hit a bump. She hadn't snooped through their stuff with her gloves off in a while. What sort of things were they not telling? Tennie pursed her lips and pushed the thought away.

She rolled her window all the way down to enjoy the view.

Wind whipped her fine brown bob. She daydreamed that the playful fog ran its fingers through her hair until her entire body turned into white wisps, and she could float around like an echo through the patchwork mountains. Far away from peanut-butter-smelling vans and cramped apartments and her wonderful, terrible family . . .

"Shoes on, everybody; we're meeting Mimsy for pizza in fifteen!" Dad barked.

Tennie didn't mind not being the one to stay at Mimsy's. She was fine.

Outside her window, the glorious woods began to thin. Down the long slope on the other side of a gully beside the road, the woods turned strange and twisted. Trees grew slanted, or even sideways before bending up again, like broken necks.

Enormous rough boulders sank their teeth into the scarred ground that was red as a skinned elbow. The mist wound a swift course around them, as if trying to spell its name in cursive.

"What happened to you?" Tennie murmured to the battered slope.

The van slowed as it neared a switchback, giving Tennie the chance to study the nearest crooked oak tree. At least, Tennie thought it must be an oak; its leaves were long gone, maybe even ages before autumn had begun. Only a single decoration fluttered atop the highest branches. Tennie squinted to see what it was.

As the van's tires crunched and rumbled, Tennie discovered the thing in the tree was a doll. Her rib cage zinged with a strange little excitement, and her fingers gripped the door.

It wasn't just any doll. It was *Shiloh's* doll, Mr. Fancy Pants— the one that had just been in her sister's arms minutes before but was now somehow dangling up in that shriveled-up tree. Its sightless black-circle eyes and ratty yarn hair were unmistakable. *How did it get up there?* Tennie's skin crawled from the strangeness of it. She whipped her head toward her sleeping sister, and a giggle of relief burst from between her lips. Mr. Fancy Pants was still in Shiloh's arms, wedged between her and Harper where he belonged. *Of course.*

Tennie craned her head out the van window, looking back toward the gnarled tree. The tree-doll wore a dress completely coated in fresh, red mud. It was dripping with it, in fact, as if it had just been plucked from a puddle and hung to dry. Tennie frowned as the dead tree and the doll shrank from sight. She reached for the window button, suddenly shivering with cold.

But before the glass raised completely, a blur of black and red swooped by her window. A large black bird—a crow?—flapped its wings furiously against the weight of the dirty, raggedy doll in its beak, swinging by the hair. Tennie chuckled again, nervously. *So that's how the doppelgänger doll got up in the tree.*

The crow swooped back by her window again, feathers gleaming reddish purple in the sunset. The doll's head hung limp, bent backward. Right before it flew away, Tennie almost swore she heard Harper—or was it Shiloh?—giggle and whisper, *"Stay with us."*

But when Tennie turned her head to assure her sisters she wasn't going anywhere, they were both snoring softly, still fast asleep.

CHAPTER 2

Soon, they rolled into a little valley
where shops and restaurants huddled, their windows glowing
amber and inviting. *Howler's Hollow.* Sprawling sycamores
rambled throughout the city center, and streetlights winked
between their branches. It wasn't fancy. Main Street was as
much woods as concrete, with plenty of places to wander
around and breathe. *I could go bare-handed, just for a minute,*
Tennie realized as they parked and emptied onto the sidewalk. She lingered as her siblings' voices drifted toward the
pizza shop.

Peeling off her wool gloves, she snatched an especially red
maple leaf from the ground. Tennie drew her fingertip over

its wax-paper veins, inhaling the syrupy scent. At the family's new apartment, there weren't towering trees like in the mountains. In the woods, everything was safe to touch, gloves or no gloves—trees didn't belong to anyone, so they never kept secrets. *"Stay here"* was the only thing she could imagine them saying. *"Don't leave the Hollow."*

She wished she could stay.

Her hand crept toward the tiara shard in her hoodie pocket.

"Tenn, c'mon! Food's waitin'!" Dad's voice interrupted.

He propped open the door to the pizza parlor with his Caterpillar boot, and waved her in. Tennie paused to study the pizzeria sign. Hand-painted neon green and purple letters read: PIE IN THE SKY. Warm air laden with oregano and yeast made Tennie's stomach grumble.

"Tenn!" Dad barked, laughing. "We're lettin' all the bought-air out!"

Donning her gloves, Tennie hustled inside where a zany array of sights and smells awaited her. Gnarly papier-mâché trees strung with twinkle lights sprouted from floor to ceiling between tables and booths. Wild-colored murals tattooed every inch of the cinder-block walls. Possums, blue-tailed lizards, and red wolves swirled artistically next to neon axolotls, ghost-faced bats, and armadillos. It was *busy*, but Tennie liked it.

When Tennie's senses adjusted, she spotted Mimsy in the corner. Her grandmother's silver hair towered in its signature cinnamon bun swirl, and her arms waited, outstretched. Tennie giggled and dodged a waitress in her hurry to hug Mimsy's neck.

"There's my Storybook," Mimsy cried, squeezing Tennie until her bones creaked. "Storybook" was what Mimsy had started calling Tennie when the twins were born. The twins and Birch might be the bookends, Mimsy confided, but her Tennie was a book full of wonderful secrets, if you knew how to read her right. This was fine when Tennie was six, but now she looked around sheepishly, embarrassed.

"Personal pizzas, Mimsy's treat," Dad prodded. "Menu's up yonder."

Tennie studied the funky menu board, overwhelmed. Pesto pizza, Cherokee purple tomato pie, adobo pork and sweet onion flatbread, Mexican hot chocolate . . .

Her mouth watered. "I'll have . . . a Mexican hot chocolate, please, and . . . um . . ." Why wouldn't her brain work? Usually, she just went along with whatever pizza kept her siblings happy. Cheeks hot, she couldn't make herself look at the lady taking her order. "Sorry, ma'am."

"Oh, *no*. Please don't call me ma'am," a laughing, raspy voice replied.

The lady behind the counter wasn't a lady at all—it was a kid Tennie's age. Sharp gold-brown eyes studied Tennie from under a short thatch of curly, dark hair. The kid erupted into a bright, white smile. "Need help deciding?"

Tennie nodded and tripped over the toe of her shoe. "Sure."

"My folks own this place, so I've tried 'em all. What's your thing? You in the mood for spicy, garlic, sweet stuff, vegetarian . . . ?"

"Uhh . . ."

"My grandbaby's partial to sweet eatin', like her grandma," Mimsy announced, rescuing Tennie. "On account of we're both so sweet, too." Mimsy's pearly dentures gleamed, and all twenty-five Swarovski crystal baubles on her keychain rattled in agreement.

The cute kid behind the cash register nodded solemnly, then winked. "Got it. We've got pineapple, sweet Vidalia onion, figs . . ."

Tennie wished the floor would swallow her. "Plain cheese?" she croaked. It was a safe choice. The cheapest, too.

Cashier Kid stuck their tongue out a little as they scribbled down the order. Tennie was horrified to find she couldn't seem to stop staring. She swallowed, admiring the confident flourishes of their pen. "Soda or sweet tea?"

"Sweet tea."

Mimsy reached across the counter and patted the cashier's arm. "Your folks sure are blessed to have such a good young'un, Fox."

Fox smiled and blushed. "Thanks, Mrs. Whitby."

Tennie gathered her hot chocolate and tea, then followed Mimsy over to a table where the rest of the family slurped Cokes and chattered, mouths full of pizza. There was just one chair left, and Tennie pulled it out for Mimsy to sit. As Mimsy began grilling Mama about their new apartment, Tennie searched for an extra chair. All taken. *Pie in the Sky sure is popular*, Tennie mused. The only empty spot was a booth behind the table, so Tennie settled in there with her iced tea and hot chocolate, and waited for her pizza.

One long, purple vinyl booth, all to herself.

Tennie squeezed some lemon into her sweet tea, then leaned back and sipped, rolling her eyes in relief. Peace and calm. *Look on the bright side*, she ordered herself. *Even if I don't get my own room at Mimsy's, at least I have a booth to myself, just for a while.*

Someday, Tennie promised herself, when she had her own apartment, she'd paint the walls exactly this shade of purple. She'd string up lights and have pink salt lamps and one of those tiny plug-in waterfalls. And never leave, if she didn't have to. She swallowed hard.

15

"Hey! You okay?"

Tennie jumped. Fox, the kid from the cash register, stood next to Tennie's booth, wrangling a rolling cart full of pizza.

"Sorry, didn't mean to surprise ya! Here, take this!" Fox thrust Tennie's cheese-only order in front of her with a flourish.

"Oh! Thanks," Tennie said politely.

But Fox didn't stop there. With shoves and clatters, they proceeded to unload the entire food cart onto Tennie's table. Tennie stared in shock, mouth drifting open and shut. Should she say something? What should she say? *Make words, Tennie!* Pesto pizza, BBQ pizza, sun-dried tomato pizza . . . *flop, flop, flopped* onto the table, dripping cheese and smearing sauce across the tablecloth.

Finally, Tennie's voice switched on and came out all Older Sister. "These ain't mine! I think you're givin' me someone else's order! And you're spreadin' cheese from here to Raleigh!"

"Pretty great, eh?" Fox grinned crookedly.

"But . . . no!" Tennie's heart skittered even as her nostrils flared. A whirl of mouthwatering smells made her stomach rumble despite the growing mess.

"It's my supper break! We're closin' in half an hour, so I made myself pizza before we turn off the ovens. But there's nowhere else to sit," Fox said, shrugging one wiry shoulder.

Then, as if manners only just occurred to them, Fox blurted, "Oh. Can I sit here? Do you want me to go?"

"If there's nowhere else, I guess it's fine." Tennie cautiously unfolded her napkin, warming to the idea of sharing the table. Fox *was* interesting, even if Tennie's heart was still beating out of time over the interruption.

Fox reached across the table, corralling several kinds of pizza onto their plate like they were Pokémon cards and they had to "catch 'em all."

"Sorry to barge," Fox said. "It's just I noticed we had somethin' in common."

In common? Tennie studied Fox. There were little ghosts and stars Sharpied up and down Fox's arms. Fox also had wild, curly hair that could only be described as *ecstatic*. Tennie's own stick-straight bob had never dared to tempt gravity quite like that.

"What have we got in common?" Tennie asked.

Fox plopped pieces of fancy pizza on top of Tennie's panic-order of "plain cheese," and said, "We both hate makin' decisions!"

Tennie giggled. "So you picked one of *everything*."

"Well, *yeah*! It's the only way." Fox laughed, taking a gulp of tea. "So, when did you move to the Hollow? Maybe we'll be in the same homeroom at Howler Middle! What grade are you in?"

Something twigged behind Tennie's sternum. For a second, she wanted to lie and pretend she and Fox *could* be in the same class. Instead, she made a wry face and shrugged. "I'm in seventh, but I live almost an hour up the road. And, anyway, I just do school online."

"Aw, man. Maybe you'll come stay with your Mimsy lots."

"Prob'ly not for a while," Tennie admitted. "My mom needs my help at home."

"Bummer."

They munched in silence for a minute, and Tennie kicked herself for letting the chat get gloomy. *Don't be such a wet blanket*, she chided herself. Tennie tried again.

"So, you got any sisters or brothers?"

Honest to goodness, Fox's face *glitched* like something from a video game. It was the fastest sad face Tennie'd ever seen anyone pull—there and gone—quick enough to make Tennie doubt she'd seen it. Fox touched a faded friendship bracelet on their wrist. "I'm an only."

Tennie gave them a gentle smile. "Hey, honestly? That sounds amazing."

"Right?" Fox smiled back, but it was a touch plastic. Tennie chewed a stray fiber from her glove, pretending not to notice Fox twisting their bracelet. Hiding a secret, no doubt. Thanks to her superburden, Tennie had grown a radar for these things.

I bet that bracelet's important. Bet I could find a memory in there and help Fox feel better somehow, a slithering thought suggested.

No, ma'am, she reprimanded herself. *Mind your own biscuits*. Folks had their reasons for keeping stuff private. Tennie's superpower was strictly used on a need-to-know basis, inside her own family. That kept her busy enough. Tennie sipped her tea. "D'you ever get bored living all the way out here?"

Fox shrugged. "Where did you move from?"

"Down near Athens, Georgia."

Fox waggled thick eyebrows, and Tennie's heart skippity-skipped. "Did you ever get bored in Athens?"

"S'hard to get bored with a family like mine."

"Same!" Fox laughed. "If I'm not in the restaurant, there's always something else to do in the Hollow, especially in the fall. Spelunking with my dad, bonfires, going to the Harvest Carnival, working in the haunted house, doing the giant pumpkin race—"

"Giant *pumpkin* race?"

"Grow huge pumpkins, scrape 'em out, put 'em on wheels,

and everyone races down a huge hill. Some clown usually breaks a wrist or something. It's the best!"

Tennie chuckled. She cut another bite of pizza with a fork, careful not to dirty her gloves. Fox pointed a slice of pepperoni at her. Tennie felt the casual weight of a skinny knee nudging her sturdy one under the table and flushed.

"You always eat pizza like that?"

Tennie studied Fox's expression, then relaxed. Fox wasn't teasing about her gloves—just curious about the fork. Before Tennie could make up an answer, a voice called Fox's name through the swinging kitchen doors, along with a playful-sounding string of Spanish. An icy breeze curled around Tennie's exposed ankles and neck. Fox rolled her eyes and smirked.

"Who was that?" Tennie asked shyly.

Fox quirked their mouth. "You *heard* that?"

"Yeah. Why shouldn't I?"

Fox eyed Tennie carefully, then produced a Sharpie from their jeans back pocket. "No reason. That . . . was my abuela. Apparently, I gotta go pull my dessert pizza before it turns into a pile of charcoal. Hey, gimme your arm?"

Tennie did, curious. Fox wrapped warm fingers around Tennie's wrist and scribbled something with the marker's tickly felt tip. It was a phone number, along with the words: "Fox Sanchez-Griffin," and beneath that, "Pronouns: they/them."

"For if you do visit the Hollow." Fox grinned. "Gotta go, but text me! *Don't forget!*" Then Fox sprinted away, leaving Tennie sitting alone with a table full of pizza.

Tennie's helium heart floated to the ceiling. From the jukebox against the far wall, a slick remix of "Spooky Scary Skeletons" thumped, and the twins high-fived each other over their song choice. Tennie giddily bobbed her head to the beat. She didn't even have a cell phone to text with, but that didn't matter. Someone wanted to text her. Tennie couldn't stop grinning.

Birch wandered over, eying the pizza-strewn table. "Holy heck, Tennie. Mimsy let you order all this?"

"Not exactly." Tennie blew on her arm, making sure Fox's ink dried without smudging.

"Mind if I have some?" Birch asked, a slice already half-way to his mouth.

"Help yourself," Tennie said dryly.

"Only got a few minutes till I have to go to Mimsy's," he muttered, chewing.

Tennie raised an eyebrow in surprise. "You don't look happy. I'd be dancing."

Birch frowned. "You want to go instead? 'Cause I'm fine with that. Ever since Poppy died, staying in that house gives me the morbs. Besides, the well water there smells like egg burps."

"Ew. What I want ain't the point, Birch. You should just appreciate going, is all."

"Don't tell me how to feel." Birch glowered, tossing sandy hair from his eyes. "I get enough of that from everyone else. I know what I want. And that's to tell Mimsy I'm not going." Birch stood up. Tennie knew that stubborn twitch in his jaw.

"Don't you dare! *Birch!*" Tennie hissed. "Mama's counting on you to not blow the family's cover! Mimsy's supposed to think you're excited to go help, so she don't find out about our money problems."

Birch scoffed. "So? Let her find out."

How can he be so selfish? Tennie scrambled to get ahead of her brother, grabbing his arm and swinging around him. She had to do something, or Mimsy and Mama would fight for ages. Worse, they might stop talking to each other completely, like they had the whole time Mama was blue and embarrassed for Mimsy to find out. Tennie gripped the edge of her grandmother's chair.

"Mimsy, let me come stay with you!" Tennie blurted. Her parents' heads jerked up in surprise. "I know Birch wants to, but it's even *more* important to me. And I can help out just as much as he does." She held up her inky arm. "And see? I already made a friend here. *Please?*"

Mimsy glanced at Birch. He shrugged. "Works for me."

"Well, I guess that's settled, then," Mimsy laughed. "I happen to have new clothes up at the house for Tennie, and a spare toothbrush—she can use those."

Mama's lips parted in surprise, but she recovered fast. "I guess Tennie could use some time away. With her doin' online school this year, it'd be good for her to hang out with some kids in the Hollow. And take a break from Thing One and Thing Two, here." She tipped her head at the twins, who had stuck their straws up their noses. Mama looked at Dad, who gave a thumbs-up.

Then, while Mama and Mimsy argued over who got to leave the tip and Dad collected leftovers into a take-out box, Tennie playfully herded the twins out the door. But her heart was in her throat. Had she done the right thing? As they exited the pizzeria, another stream of ice-cold air kissed her neck— probably from a hidden AC vent—making her shudder.

They all walked down the sidewalk toward the cars, Tennie lagging behind with her brother and wringing her hands. "Birch, you have to help Mama and Dad. I know you don't usually, but remember how Mama got last time she was really stressed out? She let the garden die. She barely talked for months, Birch."

"You know I'm not a moron, right, Tenn? Obviously, I remember."

"You can't let that happen. Promise."

He sighed. "Fine. I promise. Here, take my phone, hero." Birch pressed his cell into Tennie's palm, along with a charger.

Tennie softened. "You sure? How will you listen to music?"

"I'll borrow Mom's. It's creepy up on the mountain alone. You need a way to call."

In the parking lot, crickets creaked mournfully from the bushes as everyone said their goodbyes. Mimsy kissed the twins, and Mama threw back her head and laughed as Dad whispered a joke in her ear. The happy, deep-belly sound of it filled Tennie like warm cinnamon tea.

"Don't disappear again, Mama," Tennie whispered as they waved bye. *"I'm sorry I'm leaving."* It was only half true. Part of Tennie was thrilled to go.

Wind rustled the leaves overhead. *"We're glad you're staying,"* they said.

Then, Mimsy drove Tennie, sleepy and full of pizza, deeper into Howler's Hollow and up the dim, twisting dirt road to Mimsy's mountain home. And all the way there, in the corner of her eye, Tennie kept imagining glimpses of twisting mist and black, beating wings.

CHAPTER 3

The next morning, Tennie stretched her limbs out, out, out into a star shape and gloried in the coolness of Mimsy's clean, cedar-stored bedsheets, and blankets patterned in candy corn and bats. *Bet Mimsy's been up for ages already*, she thought. Tennie was usually up with the birds, too. Funny how well a person could rest when they weren't pounced on by feral five-year-olds before a rooster could scratch his butt. With a lazy arm, she grabbed for her borrowed phone and flipped it open. The glowing screen read 9:30.

Tennie checked her texts—the first time in her life—and saw they were from Birch.

hey, T

u up?

I'm babysitting while M and D run errands

the twins r buck wild

Shiloh dropped glass on the floor

they won't stop running around

Tennie suppressed a wicked giggle, then her belly tightened in guilt. True, it felt good to know her older brother was pulling his weight for once. It felt even better to know that he stank at it. But what if someone actually got hurt? Or needed stitches? That'd cancel out the good she did, offering to stay at Mimsy's. Making things less stressful for her parents was the entire point of leaving.

A question bubbled up in her brain. *Did you leave to help, or did you really just escape?*

Tennie kicked her covers away grumpily. Obviously, she'd wanted to keep Mama and Mimsy from fighting. That was helping.

The bubble-thought argued: *Or, you're helping yourself to some peace and quiet. There's only so much a body can take, after all.*

Tennie frowned. Even if that was true, she couldn't stop

picturing the twins running around like barefoot hooligans across broken glass. Shivering, Tennie padded across the room and yanked on a soft pumpkin-colored sweater from the dresser, along with some jeans from Mimsy that still had clearance tags attached. Then, she texted Birch back.

Keep them still.

do u want me to call & tell them a story?

Its fine
bribed them still w little debbies

"For *breakfast*?!" Tennie screeched out loud.

"What's that, precious?" Mimsy's voice floated down the hall.

No way was Tennie going to tell Mimsy her slouchy brother was home alone with the twins, sweeping glass and feeding them snack cakes for breakfast. Mama would *die*. "Be right there, Mimsy!" Tennie sang, then frowned and texted:

Just give them a movie until m and d get home!! no more sugar!!

Hurrying, Tennie tied her shoes, pushed back her sweater sleeves, then wiggled her fingers into their woolen prisons before hurrying downstairs. Her stomach roared as the smell of cider, sausage gravy, and biscuits swirled around her, welcoming her to the kitchen. Mimsy looked up from cutting a mountain of coupons and grinned until all her teeth showed. "Morning, Storybook! Eat up! I've got a surprise for you later."

Tennie yawned and helped herself to breakfast. "Yes, ma'am. It's Rook Night, isn't it?" Mimsy had loved playing Rook—a complex card game—with her gossip circle for as long as Tennie could remember. Rook Night usually meant drool-worthy desserts. "What's the surprise? Peach cobbler or apple stack cake?"

"No Rook tonight, though I reckon I'll make a cake anyway. The surprise isn't a what, it's a *who*," Mimsy said. She got up and raised the window above the sink. Tangy, cool air slithered through the frame, crossing the warm kitchen and licking Tennie's ankles where she'd cuffed her jeans. Mimsy plucked a floral teacup from the cupboard and set to brewing. "A kindly, *special* 'who.' "

Tennie said a quick grace, then took a bite of steaming, salty biscuit. This was a perfect moment, and Tennie could do without surprises. But watching her grandma scurry around in her neatly pressed slacks with a stare like a wide-eyed hoot owl, Tennie couldn't deflate her excitement.

"Who, then?" Tennie asked, flicking crumbs from her sweater.

"Well now, don't get mad," Mimsy instructed, settling regally at the table with her tea. Mimsy was the only woman in the Hollow who took *hot tea* for breakfast instead of coffee. And always in a bone china teacup. Mama called it fussy. Tennie thought it was classy and adored it. *When I have my own house someday*, she thought, *I'll have a shelf full of teacups.*

"Why would I get mad?" Tennie asked.

"Well, your mama won't approve of me introducing y'all yet, prob'ly. New relationships can be so tricky . . ." Mimsy hemmed and hawed.

"New . . . relationships?" For one terrible second, Tennie worried Mimsy was playing matchmaker for her. She did that sometimes. Tennie's cheeks flushed.

"I'm *seeing* someone," Mimsy announced, her gray eyes shining. "I've met a nice fellow. I'd like you to meet him."

Tennie almost dropped her fork. "Oh!" The word exploded forcefully. Mimsy didn't seem to notice.

It's been five years since Poppy died, Tennie scolded herself. *That's plenty long enough.*

"Does Mama know yet?"

"Oh, I'm sure she won't care. She's not much interested in my goings-on. It's your feelings I'd love to hear about."

For several seconds, Tennie was a dizzy librarian arranging

secrets on the shelves of her heart. Mama's blues got worse right after Poppy died. *How will she react to a stranger taking his spot at the table?*

Tennie wanted to tell Mimsy that, inside, Mama was more like a fragile teacup than the stainless-steel travel thermos she liked to carry with her. But Mama's depression was a Lancasters-only secret, and the Pride Wars between Mama and Mimsy allowed for no spies or informants. It was best to remain as neutral as vanilla ice cream.

Her own feelings were lost in a tangle. Mimsy's polished nails tinkled against her teacup, and she gently tilted her coiffed gray head to the side. "Are you in a kingdom far, far away, my Storybook? You've got a dreamy look about you."

Tennie laughed and lied. "Sorry. Just thinkin' about cake. I think your news is great, Mims."

"I'm proud to hear it." Mimsy smiled, clearly pleased.

Tennie held off worrying, at least until she met Mimsy's beau. No sense borrowing trouble.

Mimsy finished her tea and busied herself at the counter by the sink, sorting a box of antiques for her flea market business. Her airy humming was punctuated by a family of crows outside in the garden, cackling to one another with gritty throats. Tennie smiled.

"You got online schoolwork to do today?" Mimsy called absently.

"Nah. It's Fall Break," Tennie said, standing and gathering her dishes. When she got to the sink, she noticed it was empty. "Mimsy, did you eat?"

Mimsy waved a hand. "I wasn't hungry. Too much to do."

Tennie raised an eyebrow—Mimsy never missed breakfast. Come to think of it, Mimsy hadn't bought herself a pie at the restaurant last night, either, but Tennie changed the subject politely. "I like your crows."

"Oh, those greedy Jaspers? They've been peckin' at my late tomatoes all week. I finally went ahead and gave 'em a bucket of mildewed peanuts."

Tennie slid her plate into the sink and leaned her elbows on the counter.

"Need me to help out with anything?"

"If you've got your heart set on it, I reckon you could scrub your plate."

Tennie heaved a contented sigh, turned the tap, and switched out her wool gloves for a yellow rubber pair. Mimsy glanced at her sideways.

"You still wearing them gloves all the time?"

Tennie tensed and tried to sound casual. "Uh-huh."

"Huh. Can't understand young'uns' fashion these days. Means I'm gettin' old, I reckon. That pair's getting shabby, though, don't you think? Maybe we'll look through my closets tomorrow and find you some vintage ones."

"I'd like that."

Bullet dodged, Tennie thought. She scrubbed as Mimsy polished old jewelry and wiped down figurines. Occasionally, Mimsy held up a sparkly bauble and placed it on the sunny windowsill for them both to admire.

"Caw-RAW!" A flutter of black feathers and a gentle *thump* at the open window made Tennie yelp. One of the garden crows landed right in front of them! It strutted across the sill on wiry toes and blinked his glittering eyes at Tennie, who held perfectly still, entranced. It was uncanny how much it favored the crow from the woods—the one with the muddy doll. But then, how would she tell the difference? For a moment, a breathless magic filled the space between them.

"Well, look-a-there," Mimsy whispered to Tennie, smiling.

The bird stared at them with cool eyes for several long moments. Gradually, Tennie formed the distinct and uncomfortable impression that the bird was deciding something about her.

I know your deep, dark secrets, he seemed to tease. *I see you, Tennie Lancaster.*

Tennie couldn't abide rudeness. *Oh no you don't*, Tennie thought. *You've got no right to interrupt my morning and judge me.*

The crow hopped uncomfortably close, bobbing its head.

"Alright, shoo!" Mimsy barked, waving a hand. "I've got plenty of crow's feet already."

It ignored Mimsy. *"Caw, caw, caw!"* He was enormous, up close. Tennie's hand inched toward the sink hose.

Before she could give him a good drenching, the crow leaned down and plucked one of Mimsy's flea market baubles—an antique, silver pocket watch—and whooshed off into the cool morning, the watch swinging lazily from his obsidian beak. His friends cackled in congratulation, and the entire murder evacuated the garden and settled in some nearby pines.

"My watch! Darn your eyes, you mean ol' rascal!" Mimsy cried, hurling a wooden spoon through the window. "That watch is not for you!" Tennie's mouth fell open as Mimsy continued to holler through the window frame. She'd never even heard her grandmother raise her voice in anger, and right now her Mimsy was yelling some rather unladylike phrases.

Finally, Mimsy slammed the window shut and let her shoulders sag, eyes watery. "That bird has excellent taste." She looked shorter and older to Tennie, who squirmed with discomfort. She looked away, more than a little embarrassed.

Time to start bein' useful around here, Tennie thought. If she retrieved Mimsy's watch, the wrinkles in the day would iron themselves out.

"I'll get it back," she blurted, slipping back into her wool gloves.

"You can *try*," Mimsy sighed, wagging her head. "But I wouldn't hold your breath."

"How hard can it be? That crow's bound to get bored and drop the watch sometime. Maybe I can make him let go."

Mimsy sighed again and yanked her recipe box and a sack of flour from the cabinet. "*Good luck*. Don't be gone more than an hour, darlin'."

Tennie borrowed a pair of Mimsy's old hiking shoes—they were only a half-size too big for her, and it beat mucking up her canvas ones—and donned her jacket from the hallway closet. She filled its pockets with several tennis balls and dashed out the front door onto the wraparound porch, hoping to sneak around the house and take the crows by surprise.

"Alright, mister," she whispered, tiptoeing across the wooden boards. "Time for an ambush."

She sneaked down the porch stairs and edged along the tree line into the backyard, spotting the murder of crows. Her gloved fingers curled around one of the fuzzy tennis balls in her pocket, and she calculated how near to get to nail the thief with it. *Just a little bit closer . . . slow, now . . .*

"CAW! CAW! CAW!"

The sentry's call of warning came from high in a pine behind Tennie. Right away, the crow with the pocket watch turned and noticed Tennie. He tipped his head. *Took you long enough to come after me.*

Then, lazily, he extended his wings and *flap-flapped* himself into the air, as unhurried as Birch getting ready for school. The rest of the crow's family rose from their perches, too, turning one by one to the forest behind Mimsy's yard.

"Oh no you don't," Tennie gasped.

But they did. They soared through the twisting trees, leaving Tennie with no other option than to follow them, completely at their mercy.

Tennie paused just inside the woods and shivered. The warm embrace of the sun abandoned her beneath the luminous canopy of orange and red, like it was too afraid to enter. Inside the forest, the Hollow was a different world. This was the realm of wild things, and now Tennie felt like the intruder and thief.

The words of one of Poppy's old Halloween songs drifted through her mind, its playful rhythm supplying a quick pace for her feet and prodding her on.

*When that ol' October storm comes a'howling down
the river,*
What will the waves wash up next?

*It'll wash up a witch, and she'll chase you with a
switch!*
That's what those ol' waves will wash up next.

It's a spooky adventure, she told herself. *And it's a perfectly safe one. Folks have walked these woods for thousands
of years.* Mimsy's property was a rare, old-growth forest,
Dad said. Some of the trees were over four hundred years old.
Tennie tried to imagine all the things they must've witnessed.

"Does it bother you?" she whispered to the trees. "Knowing
so much?"

They rustled in response: *Come and see.* A waterfall of
tingly chill bumps traveled across her scalp, then baptized her
shoulders and back. Tennie swallowed hard.

I told Mimsy I'd get her watch back, Tennie thought. A
promise was a promise, after all. *Besides, trees never tell me
their secrets.*

Tennie drew a breath and took the first step.

CHAPTER 4

Tennie stumbled after the crows, only half mindful of jutting roots and rocks buried under the carpet of leaves.

"Caw! Caw!" Keep up!

The birds weren't in any particular hurry. It seemed to Tennie that when she fell behind they stopped and waited for her to catch them before flapping ahead again. *So thoughtful,* Tennie thought dryly. *Thieves with pretty manners.*

Tennie, never one for running, nursed a mean stitch in her side as she jogged toward a deep russet oak where the crows now perched. They quirked their necks at her, bobbing softly as the branches caught a breeze. And there was the ringleader, still pinching the chain of Mimsy's watch in its beak.

They were too high for Tennie to properly aim at. Her jacket clung heavy and uncomfortable against her sticky skin, and she growled in frustration. Judging from the heat in her cheeks, her face had gone candy-apple red.

"That watch is for the flea market, you know! I hope your beak cramps. I hope your jaw's sore for weeks," Tennie shouted between breaths, allowing her jacket to slide off in a heap.

With delight, she noticed how nicely the forest swallowed her voice. The woods buffered her from the world, scouring away her ugly thoughts like a Magic Eraser as soon as she spat them out.

I could say anything out here, and only the birds would hear me, Tennie realized. For that matter, she could take off her sweaty gloves, too. With a giddy laugh, she peeled the wool from her hands and discarded them atop the rumpled jacket.

"I hate algebra!" she hollered, right from her belly. "Dad's famous lasagna is soggy as heck! Birch thinks he can sing, but he couldn't hold a pitch if it had handles!"

The crow wasn't impressed. His tail feathers swished. *So?*

"You don't know who you're dealing with, buddy," she called up into the tree.

"CAW, CAW, CAW."

"I have honest-to-grits superpowers. Two sets, really, if you count keeping secrets."

"CAW, CAW, CAW."

"*No,* I won't tell you what my other power is, nosey. That's none of your beeswax. Just give me that watch like a nice crow, and we'll forget the whole thing ever happened. Deal, Birdo?"

"Her name is French Fry," called a scratchy voice behind her.

Tennie yelped and spun, hands to her blazing cheeks.

Fox hurried through the trees toward Tennie, grinning and carrying a small white box, like the kind you get at a bakery. Their gold-brown eyes danced like they were thrilled to find company so deep in the woods. Tennie swallowed. How much of her conversation with the crow had Fox overheard? Judging by the music blaring from Fox's AirPods, not much.

Tennie struggled to switch gears as Fox stuffed their earbuds into the pocket of their purple jeans. "That crow's name is *French Fry?*"

"Well, that's what I call her, 'cause she loves to eat 'em. Don't you, girl?" Fox made kisses up at the bird, then grinned at Tennie. "Need help getting that watch back?"

"'Fraid that's a lost cause. I've been trying for an hour," Tennie huffed. "She won't get close enough to hit with a tennis ball."

Fox winced. "Luckily for you!"

"Lucky how?"

"Crows have big brains, so they remember people's faces. They hold grudges longer than lines at Disney."

"CAW-CAW!" French Fry agreed from the oak tree.

Tennie narrowed her eyes grumpily. "Their heads look pretty small to me, so their brains can't be that big."

"Are you kidding? They're huge for their body size! It's a ratio thing. They're smart *and* they can fly, so who's winning here?"

"Me. I'm afraid of heights," Tennie retorted, struggling to keep from smiling.

Fox giggled. "You're funny."

Am I? Tennie thought, heart skipping. "So how do we get the watch back?"

Fox's eyes brightened. "Here, do what I do!" They plopped their white box down on the forest floor, then settled beside it, cross-legged. Tennie raised an eyebrow but followed suit. Sitting beside Fox, Tennie caught a whiff of sweet oregano and lavender fabric softener from their bright green flannel shirt. *I probably reek of sweat*, she realized, squirming.

Fox reached for the white box and deftly flipped open the lid. Inside was a gigantic homemade cookie—not the doughy, waxy, hockey puck sort you got from a mall, but a lovely, buttery, crisp-at-the-edges *cookie*. Spelled out in giant, wobbly letters made of gummy bears, red licorice sticks, and cinnamon candies was the word "FRIENDS?" Fox grinned. "Like it?"

"Is this . . . s'posed to be for *me*?" Tennie asked, ears warming.

"Can be, if you want it! But right now, it's French Fry bait. Here, take a piece and make a big show of eating it!"

Tennie accepted happily. The buttery sugar melted in her mouth as she nibbled, exactly the way a good cookie should. "Mmmmmm, so delicious!" she said loudly through crumbs, then whispered to Fox, "for real, it's good."

"Thanks."

"But why are we doing this?"

"I feed French Fry from my back porch," Fox explained softly. "Peanuts, french fries, cookie bits. I've done it for a couple years now. When she likes the food, she brings me gifts."

"Gifts?"

"*If* she likes the food," Fox reiterated. "So she might trade some cookie for your watch. But you've gotta relax your body language, so she knows you're safe. Picture something nice and calm, like a slow Ferris wheel."

"How's that supposed to help? Afraid of heights, remember?" Tennie whispered.

"Whatever chills your grill, then."

Tennie chewed slowly and tilted her head back. Time moved sluggishly and sweetly as sunbeams found cracks in the shivering dome above, sprinkling light down on them like glitter.

"This place," Tennie realized aloud. "This place calms me down."

"Good. 'Cause French Fry knows what grouchy faces look like. They make her nervous."

Tennie snorted. "Then she should knock off stealing people's watches." But she relaxed her eyebrows and unclenched her jaw. If she got any calmer, she'd be asleep.

Then, Fox broke off hunks of the giant cookie and spread them out on the ground. French Fry took her sweet time, cocking her head. Finally, she spread her wings and swooped to the forest floor, a cautious distance away. Her feathers gleamed like polished jet, mesmerizing Tennie with every movement. The rest of French Fry's family shouted cackles of encouragement.

Tennie's breath caught as the bird hopped closer, silver watch swinging. Fox cut their eyes over to Tennie, flashing a contagious smile. *It's working!* Tennie nodded in agreement, heart thumping.

Then, easy peasy lemon squeezy, French Fry dropped the watch and attacked a big chunk of cookie, gobbling it down. Tennie inched her shoe forward and dragged Mimsy's watch toward herself. Success! She smiled from ear to ear. The long hike had been worth it.

"That's a fair trade, huh, girl?" Fox crooned.

Just as Fox raised a hand to Tennie for a high five, French Fry plucked Tennie's balled-up gloves from the ground. Screaming in triumph, she flew off into the trees with the rest of the murder in tow.

"That's . . . wha—THIS REALLY AIN'T A PAWNSHOP SITUATION!" Tennie sputtered, scrambling to her feet. "BRING THOSE BACK!"

"Least we got your watch back," Fox offered apologetically. They reached out to finish the high five, and Tennie missed, her hand grazing Fox's wrist instead. In the split second her fingertips grazed Fox's friendship bracelet, a short shock of memory woke in it and rushed at Tennie's senses. It was a powerful one.

Sadness. Tears falling and dripping from a chin. Soft crying.

Accidental snooping! Tennie jerked her hand away, trying

44

to mask her discomfort with a nervous laugh. "Oh my god, I'm so clumsy."

Fox grinned, then got to their feet and lifted the watch by its chain. It sparkled and spun a few inches from Tennie's face. Behind it, Fox smiled at Tennie with buoyant ease. Like they were already good friends.

Tennie's hands felt naked. Without her gloves, she spun into an embarrassing panic. *I can't accept the watch without gloves on. What if I wake a big memory?*

"You okay?" Fox's voice seemed muffled and far away.

Tennie nodded and forced a smile. The watch danced on its chain, glinting wildly in the light. Fox's smile dissolved to confusion, and Tennie realized she looked ridiculous standing there like a stump.

Just take it, something in her heart demanded. *Fox is waiting. So take it.* Tennie hesitated. This wasn't careful. It was begging for trouble. Every time she'd ever quietly snooped memories at school, she lost friends. It was hard to know folks' secrets without acting weird after. *But it's a* stranger's *watch, which hardly counts as snooping*, the stubborn part of her insisted. And not accepting the watch might make her lose Fox, too. She could smile right through the memories, so Fox wouldn't suspect Tennie's strangeness. Shivering hard, Tennie slowly reached out and let her bare fingers wrap around the watch's cool, smooth surface.

I don't want your dang secrets, watch, Tennie thought bitterly, imagining a tough armor around her skin.

She felt a jolt of electricity as her bare skin pressed against cool metal, but other than that, nothing happened. Tennie exhaled heavily and shuddered in relief. Was that it? Had she actually bossed her own superburden? *Or maybe the watch never had stuck memories to start with*, she thought. Plenty of objects didn't. Only strong memories got trapped. Either way, she'd gotten off lucky, it seemed. So why was her stomach still in knots?

"Wanna hang out?" Fox asked. "'Cause I was thinking about going swimming!"

Tennie laughed in surprise and shivered. "Swimming? We'd freeze our toes off! How about carving some jack-o'-lanterns inside the nice, warm—"

"Holy whoa," Fox interrupted in a low voice, staring at their shoes. "Do you see that?"

Tennie dropped her gaze. All around their feet, the edges of the fallen leaves were hardening white with bitter frost, which spread outward in a circle of premature winter. Fox's teeth began chattering, their wide eyes searching Tennie's as though she had any idea what was happening. Tennie looked back in bewilderment as puffs of frozen breath escaped her lips.

The watch burned cold in Tennie's hand like a lump of ice. Branches around them cracked as their sappy veins froze hard. "This ain't right," Tennie whispered. Her heart raced, full throttle. "I don't like it."

Fox edged closer and pressed against Tennie's arm. Their voice shook with excitement. "Do you believe in ghosts?"

"Why would you *say* that right now?" Tennie snapped.

"Well, do you?"

"Like Casper, the nice, sweet, *helpful* ghost?"

"Sure," Fox murmured. "Like the nice, helpful ones."

"Maybe. Why?" Tennie pressed her shoulder tight into Fox's skinny ribs.

"I think we woke one up. Look over there," Fox whispered, swallowing.

"I don't see anything," Tennie said stubbornly. Because it was true. But she could *feel* it, like the rattling feeling that happened when you stood too close to giant speakers at a ball game—a rumble you felt in your guts more than a sound you heard. There was something cold and dark and very *right-over-there*, and it meant for them to feel it.

Leaves began to skitter and twist across the forest floor.

PLUNK.

Tennie shrieked and Fox jumped as the invisible thing hit the ground right in front of their shoes. It scraped a fast, straight line across the frosted pine needles, moving away from them like a great cat clawing one sharp nail through sand or an unseen hand that had grabbed and only barely missed.

"What the heck?" Tennie yelped and stumbled back, her skin still alive with electric prickles. "Did you see *that*?"

Fox swallowed hard, eyes wide.

A breeze picked up and gently lifted Tennie's hair. It combed its long fingers in and out of the branches of the trees, groaning in slow anguish, like it was searching for something it knew it would never find again. *Gooooone*, it said without saying. *All gone!*

THUNK. Something hit the frosty ground a little to their right, then scratched a skinny line across the forest floor as it was dragged away again.

We gotta get out of here, Tennie told herself, but her feet wouldn't listen. She clutched the back of Fox's flannel shirt instead, choking on the words stuck in her throat. Finally, she managed a whisper. "D'ya think we should run for it?"

Fox had the audacity to give Tennie a tense grin. "If you really want to." Tennie's jaw dropped. They were *enjoying* this.

A tiny part of Tennie was, too. "Can you see it?" Fox asked, pointing over Tennie's shoulder. "Right *there*."

"What? No," Tennie whispered, trembling. She wasn't sure she wanted to see. But part of her pounding heart worried Fox might think she was a big baby if she didn't try. She strained and finally *heard* something like the wind howling, but much, much deeper. *It's the sound of nothing*, Tennie thought. *A very hungry nothing*. Like despair. Like Mama's blues, times a thousand. "I can hear it."

"Take my hand?" Fox whispered.

Tennie swallowed. Her superburden didn't work on people, but her pulse doubled anyway, at the thought of holding Fox's hand. She hesitated, then pressed her palm into theirs.

Fox's warm fingers cupped around Tennie's and squeezed. That melt-in-your-mouth, comforting-cookie feeling filled Tennie's chest, mixed with a tiny electric zing. But she couldn't enjoy it for long, because the hungry, lonely wind began to sound like words.

Empty and dead, the cavernous voice yawned, roaring through the trees in front of Tennie, beside her, then behind her.

Bite, *bite*, the voice rumbled through Tennie's rib cage. *Not a single bite.*

"Now look again," Fox croaked. "Just over there."

And just a little up the wooded hill, Tennie saw it.

Or rather, she saw what wasn't. There was a void in the woods, a spot full of deep, colorless nothing. It was roughly person-shaped, and Tennie knew without doubt that it was angry, with a gravity to rival the Earth's. The hollowness of it pulled on Tennie's gut like a black hole.

It was emptiness.

Come here, it rumbled.

"Aw, HECK no!" Tennie heard herself screaming. Her feet roared to life. A small, determined bulldozer, Tennie plowed a path straight through the underbrush, dragging Fox along with her in an iron grip. Tennie's jaw set and her legs fired to the rhythm of her terrified heart. *Nope-nope, nope-nope, nope-nope.*

Fox's shoe caught a crumbling log, and they both hit the ground, like heavy flour sacks. *"The wind's . . . knocked out of me . . ."* Fox wheezed.

Without blinking, Tennie hoisted Fox to their feet by their shirt and blazed onward, fueled by fear and spite for the evil, hungry nothing. It wasn't until the two of them charged out through a clearing onto a dirt road that Tennie realized that Fox was laughing through bouts of coughs.

"We left the cookie . . . and your jacket . . . and your grandma's watch," they wheezed, then doubled over in hysterical guffaws.

"How can you laugh?" Tennie fumed. "That watch is hateful, and it belongs in the fires of MORDOR."

"Because of that little ghost?" Fox asked.

"No, 'cause the watch was *so* not my vibe," Tennie drawled in a chilly voice. "YES, because of that ghost!"

At the same time, Tennie and Fox realized they were still clutching each other's hand. They let go and burst into nervous giggles.

"Can I tell you a secret?" Fox asked.

Tennie nodded.

"I'm sort of . . . good at ghosts. I sense 'em stronger than most folks. I can help other people sense them, too."

Tennie wiped her sweaty palms on her now-dirty jeans, thinking. "So, when you grabbed my hand . . ."

". . . it helped you see the ghost. The other day, when you heard my abuela in the restaurant? That was her spirit—she mostly sticks around the kitchen and makes sure I don't burn the place down. I thought since you could hear her, you had ghost powers, too."

Tennie absorbed this, frowning.

"But now I'm thinking I should've explained everything first. I'm sorry." Fox bit their lip. "I got excited."

Tennie waited a hair longer than strictly necessary to sigh, "It's fine. I forgive you."

Fox winced sheepishly. "Okay. But you don't think I'm evil or something?"

"Maybe. You *do* throw pizza all over the place when you eat," Tennie joked, pursing her lips. But inside, she thought: *If you only knew.* Ghosts were terrifying, but they still weren't as unsettling as digging around in someone's private memories.

"Oh man," Fox yelped, checking their cell phone. "I forgot I have to help my mom unload groceries, or I'm super grounded."

"I should head home, too, and tell Mimsy the watch is gone," Tennie admitted.

After a rushed promise to text Tennie later, Fox bounded up the dirt road.

Tennie couldn't stop thinking about how she'd held Fox's hand and how it made her feel, even if—maybe especially because—it had come with a side of terrifying ghost. Was it bananas that she felt a little . . . *excited*?

Tennie set off in the opposite direction, a secret smile sneaking across her lips.

CHAPTER 5

"Mims?" Tennie called, stomping her boots on the mat.

"In here, Storybook," Mimsy answered from the kitchen.

Tennie hurried to the kitchen, then froze in the doorway, taking in the sight of scattered flour, antiques, eggshells, and potato peels strewn across every surface. Mimsy scuttled around in circles, cleaning. It seemed like a bad time to bring up Mimsy's missing ghost-watch—the watch that Tennie was certainly *not* going back for.

"You need a hand?"

"Bless you, darlin'. There's no tellin' how many hands I could use right now," Mimsy muttered, smearing flour across her forehead as she wound a strand of hair back into her bun. "At least a dozen."

"Is your . . . your beau coming over soon?"

"In thirty minutes, and I look like a deranged possum," Mimsy replied, sweeping potato peelings into the trash with her powdery hands.

"Then I'm your girl," Tennie announced, pressing a quick kiss on Mimsy's dusty cheek. "Run get ready and I'll clean up!" *That can make up for the missing watch*, she thought.

"The wash-gloves are back under the sink! An' pull the apple stack cake in fifteen minutes, would you? *Good girl.* Mimsy owes you one!"

Mimsy dashed from the room. Tennie found the gloves and set to hustling on the kitchen. Her life as the family glue had trained her for this moment, and now, she enjoyed a dollop of smugness as the room ordered itself around her in record time. *Queen of Clean.* After she carefully set Mimsy's famous apple stack cake on the counter, all that was left was a little stack of dirty dishes, with ten minutes to spare.

Mimsy stuck her head around the corner, surveying Tennie's handiwork and threading her earlobe with a little silver hoop. "You're a miracle worker, darlin'."

Tennie sneezed through Mimsy's cloud of lilac perfume and beamed.

"Almost done!"

"Wash these, too, while you're at the dishes, will you?" Mimsy sighed, pulling a stack of especially grimy Pyrex mixing bowls from her to-be-sorted box. "Lynnette Simmons sold 'em to me for five dollars, *bless her heart*."

Tennie whistled low. She didn't know many folks in the Hollow, but Mimsy's frenemy Lynnette was legendary. Mimsy had blessed Lynnette's heart—not nicely—so many times when Tennie was small, Tennie used to think Lynnette's last name was "Blesserheart." The Pyrex was *nice*. Tennie remembered it from Mimsy's faithful antique pricing book: buttery yellow with bold black gooseberries. It was rare, and worth a good bit of money.

"Why's Lynnette selling these?"

"Cause she's dizzy as a bedbug, I reckon," Mimsy sniffed.

Tennie plunged the smallest bowl to the bottom of the deep sink, and a wave of gray water flooded her left glove. Grimacing, Tennie pulled it off, and turned to fetch a dry one from under the sink. Her elbow clipped the next bowl in line, and it teetered on the edge of the counter.

Without thinking, Tennie reached out and caught it.

She stared at the bowl in her bare fingers, horrified. *I don't want your secrets!* she tried to tell it. But the bowl didn't listen. Mimsy's kitchen melted away around her.

A different kitchen rose around her in hazy memory shadows. Lynnette Bless-Her-Heart's kitchen, *Tennie guessed, since the curtains were Tabasco-bottle print.*

A brown face with smile lines and ruby lipstick squinted at memory-Lynnette. "You love those dishes, Lynnette Simmons. They've been your popcorn bowls at every Rook Night for years. Now, why would you give them away?"

"Roselle, I've got to. She's struggling with bills an' selling off her own jewelry! We both know she's too proud for charity. This is the next best thing."

Roselle nodded. "I'll look through my things, too, then, and see what I've got."

Tennie jolted out of the memory woozy and gasping for breath. She looked down and a sad *coo* escaped her mouth. The little gooseberry bowl lay on the floor, smashed like a fallen Easter egg.

"Well, darn it," Mimsy said as she emerged from the pantry and saw the mess.

Tennie's eyes swam. "The bowl fell when I bumped it and . . ."

Mimsy reached over the glass and patted Tennie. "Don't worry about it, sugar foot! We've still got three left. It's not like I needed Lynnette's tacky bowl, anyway." She winked.

Only you do, Tennie thought. *You need the money, and you've been lying and paying for our family's dinners, and I can't even say a word about it without giving my ability away.*

"Russell will be here in a few minutes," Mimsy announced. "Why don't you run upstairs and change?"

Tennie looked at her clothes and blushed. Mud-smeared, covered in pine needle bits and cookie crumbs, she was far from company-ready. She wiped her eyes and nodded, hustling up the stairway and down the long hall to the Halloween-themed guest room.

"Way to go, me," Tennie huffed. She shed her dirty clothes and slammed them into the hamper, then sat down hard on the bed. "First you lose the watch, then you break an expensive bowl right after you find out Mimsy's running out of cash."

Tennie fought the urge to wallow under the covers. *I could lie and tell Mimsy I've got monster-cramps*, she fantasized. *I'll skip the "meet-your-new-grandpa" supper, cry into my pillow for an hour, then sneak downstairs for cake later tonight.*

But lying would only make things worse. Then she'd be letting her grandma down three times.

Ding-dong!

Tennie's thoughts dissolved into panic. Mimsy's beau had arrived for supper, and Tennie was lollygagging in her underwear.

She dashed to her dresser and shimmied into an oversized purple sweatshirt and a pair of Mimsy's old leggings, rushed through socks and shoes, and washed her grimy face off in the bathroom. Then she tiptoed across the creaky floorboards of the hallway to the closet where Mimsy stored her old winter things. In a box labeled *Harold*, beneath reams of drawings and old paintbrushes, Tennie found a pair of stretchy wool gloves.

Taking a deep breath, she lifted them gingerly, not sure what kind of memory to expect: weak, strong, or none at all?

The wisp of a memory woke faint and sweet: the smell of autumn, the gentle scritchity-scritch of Poppy's pencil against paper, and birdsong in the forest. It felt almost like cheating—catching her grandfather's peaceful nature like the hiccups.

"Thanks, Poppy," Tennie whispered. She slid them on and hurried downstairs.

Tennie followed Mimsy's laughter into the dining room, where an older man sat at the table, lingering over coffee. He'd hitched up his perfectly pressed slacks so he could settle comfortably. Careful silver waves of hair and spicy old man cologne said he was still trying to impress Mimsy. But the two chuckled like old friends, so it probably wasn't his first time over. Something about the proprietary way he draped his arm over the chair made Tennie feel like the visitor. It annoyed her. She cleared her throat awkwardly at the doorway.

"Is this the infamous Tennessee? A beauty, just like her grandmother," the man boomed, taking the room by the reins. Each word was well-oiled and clipped neatly. *To match his beard*, Tennie observed as Mimsy scoffed in fake modesty and beamed.

"Tennie, come say hello to my friend, Mr. Russell Bolton."

"Nice to meet you," Tennie said politely, taking her spot at the end of the table.

"Oh-ho, sitting at the head of the table! This girl's going places in life, isn't she?" Mr. Bolton chuckled. He settled his coffee and raised his chin with an air of authority.

Tennie blinked, unsure how to respond. "Do you need help bringin' the food, Mimsy?"

"You've helped plenty today, darlin'. I'll just be a minute," Mimsy purred. She floated to the kitchen, glowing with hostess pride.

Tennie and Mr. Bolton sat alone. Mercifully, Whittlefish, Mimsy's ancient black cat, slunk into the dining room and broke the awkward silence with a long, hateful growl.

"Decided to come out from the bedroom at last?" Mr. Bolton asked him.

Tennie raised an eyebrow, wondering how Mr. Bolton knew where Whittlefish usually hid. Mimsy's beau extended his hand to the cat. Whittlefish stared blandly, then jumped onto the far end of the table and licked his privates.

"Um, Mr. Bolton . . . I wouldn't try and pet him, if I were you. He's cantankerous."

Mr. Bolton took a butterscotch from his pocket and untwisted the wrapper. "Wise advice. I have a healthy respect for cats," he confided, eyes sparkling. "Such brilliant opportunists."

Again, Tennie was left not knowing what to say. Mr. Bolton seemed to have strongly formed opinions about everything, which made conversation tricky. *I ought to try, for Mimsy's sake*, she scolded herself. "What do you mean?"

Mr. Bolton stood, circled the table, and leaned against it, just out of the cat's reach. "They found a way to escape nature's vicious circle, didn't they? Felines convinced us they were gods, and now we wait on them hand and foot. All that, just by using their noodles," he said, tapping his temple.

Whittlefish sauntered over, purring. Mr. Bolton scratched the cat beneath his striped chin. "You knew you deserved the best, didn't you, good feller? Little hoodwinker, tricking the silly humans."

Tennie smiled politely, not bothering to correct Mr. Bolton on the origins of Whittlefish: Poppy had found him as a flea-infested kitten behind a dumpster. Her grandpa had worked for weeks, bottle-feeding the helpless cat. But Tennie could tell Mr. Bolton meant well. Anyway, it was a good sign if Whittlefish liked a person—an honor usually hard-earned.

Mimsy strode in with skirts swishing, carrying a pot of beef-and-autumn-squash stew. As they ate, Tennie blushed and squirmed awkwardly. The couple kept roping her into the flirt-ing dance of their conversation. It was obvious Mimsy wanted Tennie to be impressed by her beau, and Mr. Bolton was doing his bit with gusto. No doubt Mimsy hoped Tennie would act as ambassador to the whole Lancaster clan on his behalf. Tennie shuttled a potato around her bowl with her spoon.

"Mr. Bolton was raised in the mountains, too," Mimsy offered.

"Do you live nearby?" Tennie sipped her tea.

"Not exactly. I travel around quite a bit for work," Mr. Bolton replied.

"He owns a place outside Asheville," Mimsy put in. "You know the place up on the cliff in Waynesville? The stone one with the copper turrets. Mercy, my cabin must feel like a broom closet to him." Mimsy chuckled.

Tennie choked mid-sip. She'd seen that place when she was little—she and Birch had called it "the castle," and imagined some powerful sorcerer must live there. "*That's* your house?"

"One of my homes, yes," Mr. Bolton replied, patting Mimsy's hand. "And, come now, dear. There's no place I'd rather be than here with you!"

"We met when I delivered antique mirrors for one of his bathrooms," Mimsy went on, smiling. "They complemented his stained-glass skylights and waterfall shower. And then we went for coffee, and I found out he was quite the charmer."

Tennie wished Birch was here to share *"Did you hear that?"* kicks under the table. She thought of her family crammed into their rental house. If they lived somewhere as big as all that, they'd never see each other, much less squabble over beds.

"Don't it get lonesome staying in a place that big?" she wondered aloud.

"As a matter of fact, it does. I've been thinking of settling down somewhere with rustic mountain charm," Mr. Bolton hinted. Mimsy blushed. "Especially a place with such an impressive view of the forest."

Who wouldn't prefer a cabin over a creepy castle? Tennie thought. Mimsy's home was perfection. It had a pulsing soul that rocked you to sleep at night and was glad to see you in the morning.

But Tennie knew what Mr. Bolton meant: He and Mimsy were getting serious. Bold talk. *But with someone like that, Mims won't ever have to worry about making ends meet again,* Tennie thought, chewing her lip.

The adults droned on about the boundary of Mimsy's woods now, and how it ran clear down the mountain and abutted a corner of the old Hearn farm. Tennie had almost dozed off when her phone buzzed with a text in her pocket. *Maybe it's Birch,* she guessed. Or even better, Fox. Tennie felt her lips curve into a smile. Maybe Mimsy would let her escape to her room.

"Mimsy, may I be excused, please?"

"Absolutely, darlin'," Mimsy replied. A little too eagerly, winking at Mr. Bolton.

Gross, Tennie thought, blocking out thoughts of her grandma canoodling. "Nice to meet you, Mr. Bolton."

"My pleasure, dear."

Tennie hauled her clattering dishes to the kitchen and plated herself a colossal slice of apple stack cake, which she smuggled upstairs.

Plopping onto her bed, she savored the spicy perfection and unlocked her phone. Three texts from Birch:

ugh I think mom's sick
she yarfed again & went to bed early
hope it's not contagious

Guilt weighed Tennie's heart, and she lowered her cake. She typed and deleted several truthful replies before sending one.

hope she feels better soon!
let her sleep in tomorrow.

I was going 2 practice the trumpet by her bed
good thing u stopped me

Tennie giggled. "Dingus," she whispered. She wanted to say: *Guess what? I saw a horrible ghost today. My skin's still crawling.* Or *I held someone's hand today, Birch.* Or *Mimsy has a new beau, and money troubles just like us.* But all the words stuck. When they were little, she and Birch had shared all their gossip. That was before the twins, though, and before Tennie's superburden kept her so busy.

She tossed her phone aside and shoveled down bites of apple cake, letting its sweet tartness bolster her courage. She should text Fox, shouldn't she?

"Okay, Tennie," she whispered. "This friend thing is easy. People do it all the time." Trouble was, she'd been out of school for a year and had spoken fluent "bossy grown-up" to the twins for months. She was as rusty as the water in Mimsy's guest sink. Should she be funny? Clever? *Best dip your toe in and test the water*, she told herself. She entered Fox's number and typed:

hey, it's Tennie.

Almost immediately, Fox texted back:

TENNIE!!!! french fry brought me another gift
a bag of old marbles
my spOoKy senses are tingling
but no ghost so far
☹ ☹ ☹ ☹ ☹

French Fry still owes me gloves

been thinking
the ghost escaped when u touched the watch

65

i think u might have ghost powers too

want 2 meet in the woods tom morning and test the theory?

Tennie's heart thumped. *Could* she say yes? She wanted to spend more time with Fox. But should she tell them about her superburden? And what did that have to do with ghosts? Tennie frowned hard, thinking. She usually only found memories in objects that had seen something too intense or important to forget. *Maybe a ghost is like a memory*, Tennie guessed, *and can get stuck in objects, too.* It seemed too bizarre, the idea of ghosts living forever inside the things they used to own. But not more bizarre than her waking them up. She shuddered.

The lonely, terrible *nothing* feeling of the one she'd seen in the forest still bothered her. But then she remembered her arm smooshed up against Fox's like they were already friends, how they'd laughed together, and how her heart had melted over clutching someone's hand.

Was it hurting anything, messing around with ghosts in the woods? What folks didn't know wouldn't hurt them. Besides, Mimsy would probably be busy tomorrow, entertaining Mr. Waterfall-Shower, who was—Tennie gagged—staying the night since "the hotels in the Hollow are so shabby." So why was her thumb hesitating on the y-e-s? Her phone buzzed with another message.

sopaipillas instead of a cookie this time
dad makes them every Sunday

Tennie grinned. Any plan involving cinnamon pastries couldn't be all bad.

Okay.

CHAPTER 6

At 7 a.m., after being startled awake by a hysterical rooster, Tennie rocketed through her morning routine, then rummaged in Poppy's old closet for outdoor gear. She found a soft, buttery canvas messenger bag, a coffee thermos, a knit beanie, and Poppy's old walking stick with the worn velvety handle. Gingerly, she brushed her fingers against each, testing them for any surprise memories hanging around.

From the hiking stick came a cheerful stepping rhythm and Poppy's deep, gravel-pit voice. The rest were all soothing echoes, their faded forest sounds overlapping and blurring together like colors in a Monet painting. Tennie smiled and brushed her eyes with her sleeve. It was all safe to use.

She marched down the stairs and wound her way through Mimsy's living room furniture and knickknack shelves, carefully avoiding her glass figurine collection. Chatter from the porch drifted in through open windows. Tennie peered through the lace curtains and saw a sensible rust-colored pickup in the driveway. One of Mimsy's friends. No way was Tennie getting roped into a Howler's Hollow gossip session—not with Fox waiting in the forest.

She tiptoed into the empty kitchen. There, she stuffed several biscuits with slices of leftover bacon and nestled them into a paper bag, stashing them in the satchel for later. Next, she filled Poppy's thermos with steaming peppermint tea, packing an extra travel mug for Fox.

A big, silly grin kept crawling across her face. Poppy's old campfire song was stuck in her head: *When that ol' October storm comes a'howlin' down the river, what will the waves wash up next?* The echoes of Poppy's positivity were rubbing off on her. She swayed and hummed, tossing a corner of bacon to Whittlefish, who purred in appreciation.

I'm happy, she realized. Yesterday morning, she'd felt content. But today, she found herself remembering October visits long ago, when she'd danced barefoot through Mimsy's kitchen, modeling her Halloween costume as Mama and Poppy chuckled and sipped dark coffee. She'd been loud and silly then, resting in her family's adoration. *That's bein' little, I guess*, Tennie told herself, sighing. Now, those sorts of days belonged to Harper and Shiloh.

But what if—just today—she let herself be carefree again? Tennie considered it. *Fine*, she decided. Just for one day, she'd indulge herself and say yes to everything that prolonged this urge to dance and hum.

Finally, everything was packed. Tennie pulled the beanie on, then squatted on the hardwood to say goodbye to Whittlefish. He rumbled like a motorcycle and padded closer. With each skulking step, he favored his front right foot, hobbling painfully. He blinked slowly at her, and Tennie clucked her tongue.

"What happened to you? You been tanglin' with coyotes? You know you're s'posed to stay inside, you ol' monster."

Whittlefish hissed by way of explanation, his yellow eyes glittering with a grudge. Tennie frowned. A fuzzy worry then tickled the back of her mind as Whittlefish growled and licked his foot, but she couldn't decide what it meant. *It means*, she chided herself, *that you're too used to worrying all the time. Stop sniffing for trouble.* She kissed the bald patch between Whittlefish's tattered ears.

"Well, stay off it, then, you big stinkpot."

Tennie scribbled a note for Mimsy, saying she'd be back before dinner, then set off out the back door.

The sky clung low and gray to the mountains, covering them like a burial shroud. Every smoky tree in the woods was fainter than the one before it—a fuzzy copy of a copy. It was hard to even see the path as she entered the woods.

Tennie's phone buzzed in her jeans pocket. She pulled it out to see Fox had sent a map with their live location in the forest, plus a text saying: "Meet here!!"

Grinning, Tennie pocketed her gloves and followed the map on her phone. *Thwump, thwump, thwump* went Poppy's walking stick. A peaceful world inside her chest uncurled in slow, lazy tendrils as she savored the hollowed-out sound of her feet padding across piled loam. Here and there, Tennie spotted a mist-slick mushroom or an industrious snail munching its way across a bed of dead leaves, and she stopped to snap a photo with her phone camera.

"Folks get sad once the leaves fall, but you don't mind it, do you, lady?" Tennie crooned.

As Tennie hiked, everything around her fluttered and crept and spun with the braided dance of living. Patterns called out to be noticed everywhere, until Tennie finally had to scold herself for dawdling. She closed her camera app and walked faster, so Fox wouldn't think she'd blown them off.

By the time her little blue dot on the map approached Fox's, Tennie was out of breath. The gurgling trickle of a creek grew louder as Tennie crossed a small, mossy footbridge, until finally she saw colored lights swirling in the fog. "What the heck?" she muttered.

"You're HERE!" Fox's voice hollered, just before they bounded out of the fog and squashed Tennie with a quick hug. Fox gestured to a pool of water in the dim light behind them. "Behold, I am the SORCERESS OF SPOOKY!"

"Sorcer*ess*?" Tennie asked, smiling shyly. She hadn't expected Fox's hug and had—to her horror—reacted by stiffening like a frozen fish.

"I'm feeling enchanting today," Fox announced, their beglittered cheeks sparkling. "C'mon, check it out!" They grabbed Tennie by the elbow and ushered her nearer to the water.

A trickling waterfall plunged into a misty pool before continuing on its way as a thin stream beneath the footbridge. And gently circling the pool were a dozen floating trick-or-treating buckets, their plastic jack-o'-lantern grins glowing orange, green, and purple. Each had a battery-operated candle inside. A neatly spaced row of rocks at the mouth of the stream kept them corralled inside the circle. The effect was glorious and eerie and totally impractical.

"Well, that's something." Tennie giggled. "What are they for?"

"It'll help us get in the right ghostly mindset." Fox grinned, circling the pool and yanking something from a large nylon rucksack. Tennie trailed after them.

"What's that?"

"A tarp!"

"Silly me. Of course. Everyone needs a tarp, naturally," Tennie drawled. "Only I left mine at home. If I'd brought it, remind me what I'd use it for, again?"

"For the tent!" Fox crowed, sitting and yanking on a pair of rubber waders. Tennie watched as Fox forded the pool, carrying a heavy duffle bag and dodging the circling lanterns, then clambered up onto the wide boulder in its center. In a flurry of energy and elbows, Fox assembled a little pup tent atop the boulder, complete with blankets, an enormous dinosaur stuffie, and a battered box of sopaipillas. Tennie pursed her lips to hide her delight.

She cupped her hands and yelled over the sound of the stream. "I thought we were hunting ghosts!"

"What?" Fox hollered, squinting across the water.

"I thought—oh, never mind," Tennie muttered, stripping off her shoes and socks. She rolled up her jeans as far as they'd go, then stepped into the freezing water. Fox whooped in approval as Tennie waded toward the rock, teeth bared in a chattering smile. "I thought . . . we . . . were huntin' ghosts."

"We will! Here, catch!!" Fox tossed Tennie a rumpled-looking towel. Tennie dried her legs and scrubbed the feeling back into her numb toes.

"Pop a squat in the tent, and we'll eat before we bust out the marbles," Fox directed, sighing in satisfaction.

"*Excuse me?*" Tennie gasped, face aghast.

"You don't . . . want to sit down?" Fox's forehead puckered.

"That—that is not what 'pop a squat' means," Tennie sputtered, rolling down her jeans.

Fox cocked a dark eyebrow. "Dude—it means, 'Here, take a seat!' What do *you* think it means?"

"It means, you know . . ." Tennie mouthed the word *pee*. "As in, 'If you sprinkle when you tinkle, be a sweetie and wipe the seatie'?"

Fox's eyes grew wide, then they snorted with peals of laughter. "If you say 'pop a squat' at Howler's Middle, it means 'Hey, this seat is free! Sit by me!'"

"Ah." Tennie buried her flaming face into the damp towel.

"You mouthed 'pee' like it was a forbidden word," Fox hooted.

"Habit," Tennie admitted. "I'm trying to break my little sisters of potty humor."

There it was again—Fox's face went sorrowful for a split second, like a cloud passing over the sun. Then, their smile emerged again like it had never left, and their eyebrows waggled. "You hungry? Sopaipillas, as promised!"

Tennie nodded and welcomed one of the pastries with greedy fingers and sank her teeth into it. They were slightly squashed, but delicious. She couldn't help but notice when Fox laughed, they had five dimples: two big ones on their deep-tanned cheeks, two little ones by their mouth, and one extra just beside their chin. *I bet*, Tennie thought, *you can tell how funny they think a joke is by the number of dimples that show.* She made it her secret challenge to say something funny enough to see all five again, but next time without mortifying herself to the bone.

"I brought bacon biscuits and tea, too," Tennie announced, unpacking Poppy's satchel. Her stomach rumbled, and for a few minutes they munched and gazed at Fox's floating jack-o'-lanterns in silence.

"So, where's French Fry?" Tennie asked, scanning the branches above.

"Haven't seen her since she dropped this on my back porch

last night," Fox said, pulling something from their windbreaker. Tennie's breath caught. It was the muddy Raggedy Ann doll she'd seen in the tree—the one that matched Shiloh's!

"I've seen that doll before," Tennie murmured.

"What's that?"

"Nothing. Just . . . your text said something about marbles?"

The tattered doll made gentle clicking sounds as Fox set it reverently on the ground between them, facedown. In the base of its neck, there was a rusty zipper sewn with crude stitches. Fox tugged the zipper gently. The noise gave Tennie the chill bumps she sometimes got when she heard wind chimes or footsteps on gravel.

Fox explained, "When I saw it, every hair on my arm stood up."

"Is that how you know? When there's a ghost nearby, I mean?" Tennie asked.

Fox nodded. "Goose bumps. And my heart races like Usain Bolt. And, here, *feel*." Fox gently took Tennie's wrist and guided her hand over the opening in the doll's head. Tennie's eyes widened. The air around the doll stung with bitter cold. Tennie exhaled hard. When the breath reached the bag, it turned to frozen vapor, encircling it like a smoke trick.

Her jaw dropped, and Fox grinned. "Spooky, right?"

Tennie nodded, leaning back. *Definitely spooky.*

"That makes two haunted things that crazy bird's brought us—I think French Fry's psychic or something."

"So, how do we find out for sure it's haunted?"

"Well, if we're right about you having ghost powers," Fox said, "then your touch will let it out of the marbles, just like with the watch."

Tennie's stomach went heavy. She decided not to explain her real gift to Fox. *They'll get weirded out and think I'm a creeper. Just let them think you're a cool ghost-hunter.* Easy enough.

But thinking about yesterday's ghost worried her. Its hungry despair had wanted to eat her, soul and all. And this doll was *off*-looking—creepier than the watch by a long shot. She twisted the ring on her pinky finger.

"Are all ghosts as awful as the watch ghost?"

Fox paused reflectively, then finally answered: "S'hard to say. Think of it like this—ghosts were people, right?"

Tennie shrugged. "Yeah . . ."

"People are different! No one's alike! So . . . no two ghosts would be the same, either. Each ghost has its own personality. This one could be awesome!"

It hardly made her feel better, but Tennie didn't want to let on she was nervous enough to hurl. "I guess."

"Just in case, though, here's the plan. My granny always said spirits don't like three things: clear water, salt, and wool."

Could've guessed the last one myself, Tennie thought. It stood to reason. When her superburden had first started four years ago, she'd tried all sorts of things to block it. Cotton gloves, leather gardening ones—she'd even coated her hands in Elmer's glue in class, once. Only wool ever did the trick at keeping trapped memories at bay. And if ghosts were memories, that made sense.

"So, we sit on this rock surrounded by water. No ghost in their right mind would want to stay here. And I sprinkled salt into the floating lanterns for good measure. Then," Fox tugged a colorful striped blanket from the pup tent, "we wrap up in the blanket my dad was so nice to lend us. We'll be ghost-proof."

A warm-tea feeling filled Tennie's heart. It felt nice, being considered. "I like it."

"Okay," Fox said, eyes serious. "The watch ghost took a minute to wake up, right? So I'll open the doll, and you stick your hand in. As soon as we sense the ghost waking up, we throw it across the pool. That way, when it finally comes out, it's across the water when it leaves the marbles. You got a good throwing arm?"

"Used to be shortstop on my softball team," Tennie admitted

with a flash of pride. *Until I quit because Mama couldn't drive me to practice, anyway.*

"Perfect! You throw it, then we make for the blanket."

"Okay." Tennie's pulse skipped like a rock on water. Fox stuck their tongue out in concentration, stretching the zipper opening with their thumbs. Tennie peered into the dirty doll. The marbles inside were chipped and old-looking, coated in smears of what looked like dried mud. Tennie hovered her hand over the opening, and instantly her skin stung with red welts from the brutal cold that poured from the doll's neck. This was *such* a bad idea. Her voice wavered as she suppressed a terrified squeak. "On three?"

"One . . ."

"Two . . ."

"THREE." Tennie held her breath and plunged her hand into the marbles. The temperature around Tennie and Fox plummeted down, down, down.

Fox's arms erupted in goose bumps, and their face contorted with excitement. "Now! NOW! Throw the doll!!"

Tennie grabbed the yarn hair and hurled the raggedy doll across the stream. When it landed on the opposite bank, marbles rolled and bounced in every direction. A few slid and plopped into the water, causing a confusion of ripples that set the lanterns bobbing.

"Time to hide!" Tennie ordered, tugging Fox into the pup tent and wrapping the woven wool blanket around them both until only their faces peeked out. She felt queasy. Queasy and *giddy*.

"You scared?" Fox whispered, cold breath rising in front of their nose.

"Naturally," Tennie squeaked, trying to sound brave. "You?"

Fox stared through the open tent flap, eyes round and unblinking. "I'll be honest—I'm a little nervous."

"*What?* You're not supposed to be scared! You weren't afraid yesterday," Tennie hissed, eyes darting around the woods.

"I think I might've miscalculated this time, just a little."

"This is ghosts, not geometry," Tennie spat. She pulled the blanket tight. "What's to calculate?"

"There might've been more than one ghost in the marbles."

A tap on the back of the pup tent made them both jump. *Flick-thump.* Something small had hit the nylon wall, then landed on the boulder outside the tent.

"It's prob'ly a falling acorn," Fox whispered, pulling the blanket tighter. "Ghosts exist on a different plane than us—they don't usually manipulate our world." They didn't sound convinced.

"Then how'd they get trapped in objects in the first place? That's physical!" Tennie hissed.

Flick-thump. Something hit the tent wall next to Tennie. Flinching and whimpering, she squirmed closer to Fox, crowding into the left side of the pup tent.

"Creepy," Fox breathed, eyes darting.

"What?" Tennie demanded. "What is it?"

Fox's fingers brushed over Tennie's palm and laced into hers, and Tennie nearly dissolved from the *deliciousness* of the feeling. For several seconds, she couldn't notice anything else but her skipping heart. But then, softly, a high-pitched giggle floated from the trees across the water.

Tennie wanted to look.

Tennie *didn't* want to look.

She looked.

A thick patch of fog gathered just by the water's edge, and Tennie's mind raced, trying to make sense of its shape. The mist swirled and thickened, and another giggle floated across the water. It sounded *young.* Then, from the woods to their left, came the giggle's twin, followed by a soft, singsong humming. It almost sounded like . . .

Like Tennie's five-year-old sisters.

The feathery giggles circled the pool, first clockwise, then the opposite direction, then all around them. Tennie could only listen, frozen in terror. She couldn't tell how many ghosts there were. She couldn't even bring herself to *move*. It felt exactly like waking from a bad dream when she was small, worried the nightmare had followed her into the real world. Yet Tennie had the unshakeable conviction that if she stayed perfectly still there under the blanket, she and Fox would somehow be safe.

Without warning, a bloodcurdling shriek came from the direction of the footbridge straight ahead—and cold dread choked Tennie's veins. It wasn't a wild screech like a monster or a barred owl. This was the sound of a little sister stepping on shards of glass; the sound of a little sister being grabbed by a stranger on the street; the sound that a little sister made when some terrible monster was cornering her and no one in the world had come to protect her. Tennie kept repeating to herself: It's a ghost. *It can't be real.* She'd nearly conquered the impulse to run toward the scream when Fox tore their hand from Tennie's, causing the sound to fade. But obviously Fox could still hear it.

Tennie watched, perplexed, as Fox grunted and clawed their way out from under the blanket, their bare feet slipping on the folded tarp as they struggled to stand. "I have to go find her!" Fox yelped.

Fox was trying to go *after* the ghosts.

Tennie grabbed Fox's arm in an iron grip. "Oh no you don't! Your hiney stays right here, under the safety blanket— that's the deal!"

"Let me go!!"

But before Fox could break free, another something hit the tent flap right above their heads. *Flick-thump.* They both froze. This time, they saw exactly what had hit the tent, because it plopped on the ground in front of them and rolled ever-so-slowly across the crinkling blue tarp toward Tennie's bare toes. Not an acorn. It was a single, muddied marble with a deep red stripe slashed right down its middle.

Fox cursed and kicked the marble into the water as peals of impish laughter circled the pool. Tennie shook.

"They were calling for help," Fox muttered. Their face looked just as surprised as Tennie felt.

"They're already dead," Tennie snapped, grabbing Fox's sleeve to make sure they stayed put. "What kind of help do they need?"

A chorus of unhinged giggles floated across the fog. Tennie shuddered again.

"I think they're *messing* with us," Fox muttered. A sharp, sad expression had camped out behind Fox's eyes, lingering long enough for Tennie to study it. She understood the shape of it right away, because she'd seen it in her mother's eyes after her blue days had passed, when Mama didn't think Tennie was watching. It was a cruel sort of sadness that twisted back in on itself, like long, thorny greenbrier vines tangled up in knots.

Fox caught Tennie staring. The sadness disappeared. With a determined grunt, Fox yanked a blue cannister of salt from their duffle bag and opened it, pouring a handful of white into their glittery brown fingers. "Get lost, jerks!!" Fox shouted, hurling salt into the air. "We don't want you hanging around us!"

A moment later, birds began to sing again. Tennie hadn't even realized they'd stopped.

Warm air rushed into the tent, and Fox sagged to the tarp, relieved. It was over.

Tennie felt steaming words building in her chest like pressure in a teakettle. She breathed and counted to ten before saying: "You can *do* that? You just tell ghosts to leave, and they cut out like a light switch—and you didn't *tell me*? And, excuse the pun, but have you lost your marbles, runnin' after them like that?"

Fox's head dropped. They mumbled something that sounded like "*I coulda sworn it was her.*" It was such a pitiful tone, Tennie's heart softened. Fox fiddled with the bracelet on their wrist. Tennie noticed and nudged Fox's knee with her pinky.

"Wanna talk about it?"

Fox sucked in a noisy breath, and the sadness was consumed by a sheepish grin. But Tennie had seen their watery eyes. She'd *seen*. "I got carried away in the excitement. Guess I should explain my spooky abilities better, huh?"

Tennie bit back her question. *Who did you think you heard, Fox?* Obviously, someone who meant a lot to them. For Fox to have been easily tricked into running toward the ghosts' voices, it must've been someone who was as important to Fox as the twins were to Tennie.

Fox noticed Tennie staring, and their ears reddened. "Want to pack up and go to my house? We need hot chocolate if we're going to make better ghost hunting rules."

Tennie shrugged.

Fox's smile flagged a little. "I mean. If you still want to do ghost hunting."

Tennie was already folding up the blanket. "Yeah, I'm in."

They packed their things in silence and waded the stream, gathering the lanterns, then put on their shoes. Just before they headed out, Fox bent to collect the scattered marbles.

"Are you sure that's a good idea?" Tennie asked.

Fox shrugged. "They don't feel haunted anymore. Whatever was in them is out now, my friend."

Tennie shivered, and they hurried up the trail toward Fox's house.

CHAPTER 7

The late morning sun burned away

the fog as Tennie and Fox cut through the woods to the dirt road that led to the Sanchez-Griffin house. Fox chattered nervously as they trudged along the road's weedy shoulder.

"D'you know a mantis shrimp can see ten times the color we can?"

"Thinkin' up colors I've never seen gives me a headache."

"But imagine! What if there's always crazy things going on around people, and they just can't see?"

Tennie shrugged. Folks missed most of what went on around them, especially when it came to each other. People waded through rivers of invisible things all the time. "Like ghosts, you mean?"

"Exactly like ghosts."

"But *you* can see 'em," Tennie pointed out.

"Sure, the same way I see colors," Fox said, sweeping a gangly arm up at the trees. "But who knows? Maybe I'm not seeing everything there is to see about the ghosts, either."

"Too bad you're not a ghost *shrimp*, then," Tennie teased. "You could prob'ly see ten times the ghostly info."

Fox laughed until they snorted—all five dimples. Tennie's heart skipped in triumph.

"All I'm saying is, we can never know everything. I like it that way. More *mystery*."

Just then, a sleek, black car careened around the bend in the road, spitting gravel and honking as it sped toward them. Tennie and Fox dived out of the way just in time to avoid being flattened. A zing of anger shot through Tennie as she coughed in the dust cloud. Fox lobbed a clumsy rock at the car's bumper.

"Watch where you're going, jerk!" Fox hollered. The fancy car sped up the next switchback, motor raging.

That's the way to Mimsy's house, Tennie thought, worried. She'd mention it later—a few of Mimsy's older friends probably needed their car keys taken away before they ran somebody down.

A crow squawked overhead. Tennie glanced up to see

French Fry and her murder bobbing in the trees above and calling to one another excitedly. *Bet they're all disappointed we didn't end up as roadkill*, Tennie thought darkly as they approached a floral mailbox.

"So *now* you show up, huh?" Fox called to French Fry. They elbowed Tennie. "Probably waiting for me to come home and feed her. This is my driveway—race ya!" Without pausing, Fox sprinted toward a small, white farmhouse with peeling paint that sat in a tidy front yard decorated in stacked stone and colorful planters overflowing with herbs and flowers. Tennie shifted her bag and jogged to the front porch.

"Shoes off at the door," Fox directed in the doorway, flinging their sneakers haphazardly into a corner. Tennie slipped hers off and inhaled deeply. Her nose was tickled with the scent of fabric softener and the heavenly sweetness of roasted corn.

Just to the left, a woman with a shaved head and an easy smile swung around the kitchen doorway. She wore an apron that read BREAKFAST OR DIE, with two sunny-side up eggs in the shape of a skull and bacon pieces for crossbones. "Lunch soon, Fox! Wash your hands!"

"Tennie's eating, too," Fox called, motioning for Tennie to follow them to a little bathroom down the hallway. Tennie arranged her things neatly beside the door, then followed.

They washed up, and soon Tennie sat at the table with Fox and their parents. *Should I put my gloves on or chance it?* Tennie wondered. They'd been off since the woods. Usually, she left them on all the time and folks thought it was a weird fashion choice. But it would look stranger than strange to put the gloves on at the table.

Here goes nothing, she decided, heart thumping. She held her breath and picked up a fork, cold sweat prickling her upper lip. Nothing happened. Tennie exhaled and smiled.

"So are you enjoying Howler's Hollow?" Mrs. Sanchez-Griffin asked, giving Tennie a kind smile. It was immediately obvious where Fox had gotten their dimples.

"Yes, ma'am!" Tennie smiled. "I especially love the woods."

"You're in good company, then," Mr. Sanchez-Griffin noted, winking at Fox. "Fox spends more time out there with Lola's crows than she does anywhere else." Tennie glanced at Fox for explanation. *Who was Lola?*

But Fox only said, "Pronouns, Pa!" then shoveled spicy pork into their mouth.

"*They* spend time in the woods, not she, babe," Mrs. Sanchez-Griffin murmured, offering Fox's dad a plate of corn slathered in butter.

"Sorry, Fox! *They.* My brain's toast. I had to balance the

restaurant books and deal with a cranky tourist yesterday. One of those slick-haired guys who loves finger-pointing and loud cologne," Fox's dad said. He puckered his face in imitation and jabbed the air with his fork. "'I said roasted garlic *and* pesto, not roasted garlic pesto, you backwater pizza peasant!' A less righteous man than me would've told the kitchen to put Limburger on his pie."

Fox and Tennie laughed. The rest of the meal was all chit-chat and joking, and when Tennie offered to help clear the table, Mrs. Sanchez-Griffin shooed her away with a pot holder.

"You're a guest. Go. Have fun!"

Tennie thanked her and tramped up the stairs after Fox.

"Your folks are nice."

"I like 'em. This is my room," Fox said, grinning. "I decorated it myself."

Every wall was painted to look like the old-growth forest, except brighter. Deep woodland shadows were now ecstatic fuchsias, and electric-green trees soared up to the ceiling, where a galaxy at night stretched from wall to wall. The style was similar to the murals at Pie in the Sky. Tennie whirled to Fox in surprise.

"You did this?"

"Yep," Fox said, puffing out their chest.

Tennie stepped closer. Beneath the paint, there were raised outlines of bunnies, like wallpaper that had been painted over. There were haphazard spatters of paint on the floor, too, but even so . . . it was fantastic. "This is beautiful. Did you do the mural at Pie in the Sky, too?"

"Me and my dad, yeah."

"My Poppy used to be a painter," Tennie murmured, idly tracing the outline of a hidden wallpaper rabbit. "He was really good, too. Mimsy used to get mad he spent so much time painting. But I've never tried. I don't have many major skills, I guess."

"You let ghosts out of haunted stuff," Fox pointed out. "That's pretty big."

That's not even half of it, Tennie wanted to tell Fox. But she nibbled her cheek instead. Would Fox trust Tennie if she confessed her memory-stealing gift? Tennie had never told anyone, because she was sure that as soon as she did, folks would treat her differently. Maybe the same way she treated them differently, once she found out their secrets.

"Speaking of which," Fox said, kneeling by the bed and sliding a shoebox from underneath, "wanna see my box of *maybe*-haunted stuff?"

Tennie raised her eyebrows. "Maybe-haunted? Can't you

tell? Seems like it'd be hard to miss." She held up her still-itchy hands as proof. "See? I'm allergic to sudden cold. French Fry's presents gave me hives!"

"I think there might be a little spooky in them," Fox said wistfully. There was that sad look again. Tennie felt an urge to throw her arms around Fox and hug it away.

Fox centered a battered shoebox on the bed and lifted the lid. Inside was a ceramic unicorn, a plastic clown cake topper, a tube of sparkly lip balm, a hair tie, and a tiny pink leather bible. Tennie frowned. These weren't old or ominous like the pocket watch or the marbles. They almost looked like what you'd find if you cleaned the cushions of the Lancaster family couch. Tennie hovered a tentative hand over the objects—none of them were cold.

"Don't touch 'em yet, though. Mom and Dad . . . they don't even like me talking about ghosts. They'd flip if we set one free in the house."

Tennie didn't want to tell Fox they probably weren't in danger of being haunted by any of these things, whether Tennie touched them or not. They were duds. But Fox's dark amber eyes were studying her with so much hope, Tennie didn't have the heart to tell the truth.

"Maybe," she said carefully. "We can't be sure, right? Not

until I hold them. But like you said, your folks wouldn't like you tryin' in the house . . ."

"Right! So wanna spend the night and camp in the back-yard? We can see if this stuff's haunted then, if your Mimsy doesn't mind you staying over."

"Isn't it a school night?"

"Fall Break!" Fox said, bouncing in excitement. "It's gonna be chilly. I'll go get blankets and marshmallows!"

Tennie opened her mouth to say "okay," but Fox was already sprinting down the hallway. So instead, she tugged her cell phone out of her back pocket and checked her messages.

One from Birch.

You bored yet?

Text soon!

Tennie smiled and typed in: *Nope* and *Okay. Love u.* Then, she scrolled through the numbers her mom had entered into Birch's contacts until she saw "Her Elegance the Queen" paired with Mimsy's area code. Tennie rolled her eyes at her mom's weird humor, and pressed call.

Mimsy answered with a laugh in her voice—she obviously

had company. "Was wonderin' when you'd call! How's my Storybook?"

"I'm good! I walked down to Fox's house. Can I spend the night?"

"I reckon that's fine! Best double-check with your mama, though. She's funny about that sometimes. But you can tell her they're a real nice family and you're in good hands."

A deep voice chuckled in the background. Mimsy covered the phone, but Tennie heard her muffled "Pshaaww, behave yourself!" anyway.

Tennie made a face. "Is someone there at the house, Mimsy?"

"Oh, it's Mr. Bolton. That rascal heard me say I loved raspberry macarons last night at dinner, and he drove all the way down to Greensboro to get me some. Isn't that something?"

Tennie could picture Mimsy's face lit up like Christmas. She couldn't help but smile, too. "That's real sweet of him. Save me one!"

"Alright, baby. You be sweet now!"

"Yes, ma'am. Love you!"

Tennie hung up with Mimsy and dialed the number titled "Tall Parent." Her dad answered, "Yellow!" Tennie's siblings shrieked in the background, and she felt her chest squeeze with the sudden ache of missing them. "Hey, Daddy. Where's Mama?"

"Takin' a nap. She's a little under the weather. I sure do miss you, baby girl. You looking forward to your birthday in a few days?"

Tennie blinked. Between crows and ghosts and awkward dinners, she'd forgotten all about it. "Yeah, I guess."

"We're thinkin' of having your cake at Mimsy's this year! We'll all hit the big Halloween festival in the Hollow. How's that sound?"

Tennie heard Fox coming up the stairs. "Sounds good, Dad! Um, so, can I spend the night at Fox Sanchez-Griffin's? They're the folks who own the pizza shop."

"A sleepover? That's awesome, Tennie-bear! Go make friends! Kick butt, take names!"

Tennie groaned. "Oh my god, Dad, *stop*. Okay, gotta go!" She hung up the phone, heart skipping.

"What'd your Mimsy say?" Fox asked hopefully, arms overflowing with blankets and Red Vines.

"I got a yes!" Tennie grinned.

"Sweet! Here, carry," Fox ordered, thrusting blankets toward Tennie. "And we can't forget this," they said, picking up the box of maybe-haunted objects. The box of *probably-not-haunted* objects. Tennie tried to look excited for Fox's sake.

"Now what?"

"Now, we feed French Fry, then set up the tent again. It's a ghost campout!"

After they tossed overripe strawberries to French Fry's murder, Tennie helped Fox carry their gear out to the backyard, and then a few yards into the woods for good measure. As she fumbled with tent rods, her nagging brain was generating worries that she swatted away like flies.

Mama's sleeping during the day again.

"Hush," she whispered.

That car that was drivin' like a bat out of h-e-double-hockey-sticks? The one that nearly ran me and Fox over? Think that might've been Mr. Bolton.

"Hush."

An' those ghosts y'all turned loose in these woods? The woods you're campin' in? You remember what Fox said. Whatever was in that creepy watch and marbles is out now.

"Hush."

Mama's napping a lot again. Dad said she's under the weather. You've got to fix it!

"I said, hush!" Tennie exclaimed, louder than she meant to.

"What's that, Tennie?" Fox said, concerned eyebrows tenting over their eyes. *Real nice eyes*, Tennie thought.

"Nothin!"

Fox was stripping bark from skinny sticks and jamming them through way too many marshmallows at once, the tip of their tongue sticking out the side of their mouth in concentration. Tennie's heart went soft. *Today is for fun*, Tennie reminded herself. And sitting by the fire, and breathing in her forest, and telling stories.

Tennie smiled. "Nothin'. Let's make that fire."

CHAPTER 8

Tennie and Fox took a whole hour to get their camp set up, and another to get a fire blazing properly. Then the two passed the time until sunset—the only acceptable time to have a campout ghost-fest, according to Fox—by playing Clunky Jackalopes, Fox's favorite card game. It was chilly enough that the cicadas had tucked away their hymnals for the year, leaving only the never-ending trill of hearty Carolina ground crickets ringing in Tennie's ears.

"Four blue cards!" Fox gloated triumphantly, slapping them on the stump they'd used for a table.

Tennie snugged a flannel blanket around her and scooched closer to the crackling fire. "I am *not* doing that dumb turkey dance again, no matter what the rules say," she replied, blowing hair from her face and reaching for the marshmallow bag. "I forfeit!" Everything inside her glowed with contentment. She jabbed a stick through her 'mallow and set to roasting it—golden perfection with a gooey inside—then savored its sweetness.

Everything was perfect. The trees swished and whispered overhead, and Tennie let the breeze kiss her fire-toasty face. She closed her eyes and rested as Fox chattered and transformed one marshmallow after another into fireballs.

"Hey, Sleeping Beauty," Fox said, nudging Tennie's knee.

Fox stood clutching their maybe-haunted-things box and wiggled their dark eyebrows conspiratorially. "Feeling spooky?"

Tennie's stomach sank, knowing Fox would end up disappointed, but she nodded anyway. "Ready as I'll ever be! Let's have the box!"

Fox gave her a pointed look. "Don't you at least want a blanket first?"

Tennie blinked. "Oh, I've already got this one," flapping the flannel around her shoulders.

"Ah, but see, that's *cotton*," Fox winked. "We need the wool one." For a second Tennie stared in confusion, then remembered: The wool keeps loose ghosts away. Ghosts Fox was sure might pour from that trinket box, soon as Tennie touched them. *Shoot, Tennie*, she thought, kicking herself. *Play along!*

"Oh my gosh, is it? Let's get the wool throw, then!"

Once they were both snuggled with their backs to the fire, Fox balanced their trinket box on their knees. "Okay. How about the plastic clown first?"

Tennie swallowed, everything inside her wincing. The tacky plastic clown wasn't giving off cold. Worse, Tennie wasn't wearing any gloves. There may not be ghosts in there, but that didn't mean there weren't memories. She'd just have to grin and bear it. "Sounds good!" She stretched out a shaky hand.

Fox dropped the clown into Tennie's palm. The world dropped away, and Tennie plunged into a memory.

It was another birthday party. Tennie saw the scene through the eyes of a birthday girl, whose small hand plucked the clown from a cake ablaze with candles. "Wait! I don't want it to get scorched," a soft voice lisped as a chorus sang, "Happy, birthday, dear Lola . . . Happy birthday to you!" Then, before Lola could blow out the candles, a younger Fox leaned in front of the cake and blew them out instead. Tears welled up in memory-Lola's eyes, and the memory faded . . .

Tennie was back in the old-growth forest. Fox's knees pressed against hers.

"Well?" Fox asked, eyes wide. "You look like you *saw* a ghost."

Tennie squirmed. Her stomach churned. These things weren't haunted, and they felt private. Tennie didn't like pilfering Fox's memories one single bit. But she couldn't very well tell Fox so without giving away her secret.

"I dunno, Fox," Tennie lied softly. "I—I tried. But I don't think they're spooky."

"Let's try another," Fox insisted, exchanging the plastic clown for the lip balm tube. Tennie suppressed a grimace, her stomach souring. She let her fingers close around the lip balm and tried to act normal.

Not-Tennie lay in a railed bed. The smell of adhesive and disinfectant and instant potatoes filled her nostrils. Tubes were taped to the tops of her hands, snaking up, up, up to a sparkling IV bag overhead. Cartoons danced and blared from a TV mounted on the wall in front of her. Mrs. Sanchez-Griffin's kind face leaned in to kiss her forehead. "Love you, Lolabear," Fox's mom said, smiling.

Tennie dropped the lip balm and wiped clammy hands on her jeans. "Not haunted," she said firmly. She shuddered and leaned closer to the warmth of the fire, guilt gnawing at her gut. Lola was Fox's sister—a sister who wasn't here anymore. *I'm an intruder*, she thought. *I don't belong in those memories.*

"That's okay, there's still a few more . . ."

"No, Fox."

"I mean, it can't hurt to check 'em all, right? We'll do the hair tie next . . ."

"Fox, *no*. I can't."

Fox frowned. "Okaaay . . ."

"I just . . . can't, alright? I'm tired. This is wearing me slap out."

Disappointment flitted across Fox's face, but they nodded slowly. "I'm sorry, Tenn."

Tennie's eyes stung. "You're not mad, are you?"

"No way! No means no! If you're done—" Fox made a flat-pancake gesture "—you're done. Sorry for pushing. Anyway, we still have hot dogs, right?" Fox tried for a smile.

Tennie nodded, grateful. For a while, they quietly roasted hot dogs as darkness unrolled itself across the mountains and stars blinked open their eyes for the night. Then, they settled onto sleeping bags in the pup tent, leaving the flap open so they could stare at the shimmering constellations that peeked through the canopy of trees.

Fox jabbered for a while, identifying stars and pointing out the pictures they formed in the sky.

"Ain't it funny, how all the constellations have stories?" Tennie murmured.

"How do you mean?"

Tennie dug deep for words. "We see them like they're pictures on a page. And then we tell stories about what they mean to each other. Like Orion the hunter. But really, those stars are a thousand light-years away from each other. They only *look* like they belong together."

"I guess."

"I wonder if they get lonesome."

They lay quiet for a few minutes.

"Are you lonesome, Tennie?"

"Not right now."

"Me, neither." Fox's voice was a little husky.

Tennie worked up the courage to whisper, "Fox, why's it so important that those things be spooky?"

"Just curious, I guess." That was obviously a lie. Tennie felt the light-years stretch between her heart and Fox's.

Fox traced the seam of the nylon tent. "I'm tired of talking. Wanna play a game instead?"

Tennie fought against a sigh. "Sure."

"I'll trace something on your back, and you guess what it is. We'll take turns."

Tennie knew the game—she'd used it to lull Harper and Shiloh to sleep since they were toddlers. Only she was always the one drawing, and hardly ever got a turn as the drawee. She smiled in the dark. "Okay."

Fox traced a finger across the back of Tennie's shirt, drawing zigzags around her shoulders and spine. Tennie shivered with happy goose bumps, guessing long after she knew the answer. "The mountains."

"Yep! My turn."

Tennie set to work drawing a mental masterpiece across the back of Fox's T-shirt, brow knit in concentration. Finally, Fox shook with laughter. "Hey, Picasso, too many details!"

"Sorry—startin' over!" Tennie made the outline simple this time: head, wings, feet, beak.

"A hideous bear."

Tennie snorted. "NO."

"A scarecrow?"

"Closer."

Fox yawned. "A bird? French Fry."

"Ding ding ding!"

"Winner winner, chicken dinner . . ." Fox's voice trailed off drowsily. Their dark head sank into their pillow.

"G'night, Fox."

Tennie snuggled deeper into the blanket, toes still numb from the chilly night air. She listened to the crickets for a while, uncomfortable on the cold, hard ground. Fox's breathing was deep and even, but Tennie couldn't get warm. She was starting to regret agreeing to a campout when she had a perfectly soft bed at Mimsy's. She grunted in frustration.

"Shhhh," came a whisper behind her.

"Sorry," Tennie mumbled, shivering. She sneaked her feet over to steal Fox's warmth.

A happy shiver tickled up her shoulders as a gentle finger traced down her back in a long line. She sighed. "Thanks. That helps." Another snaking line trailed down her left side, and one on the right. Sloping strokes brushed her skin, and every hair on Tennie's arms prickled in delight. It reminded her of when her mama used to play with her hair. Her eyelids grew heavy.

"Mountains?" she guessed.

"No."

"Houses?"

"No."

"I give up," Tennie murmured dreamily.

"It's the forest," came the feathery reply.

"Good one," Tennie said, turning her head back toward Fox. But Fox was already sound asleep.

CHAPTER 9

Tennie slept poorly–or flourished

at tossing and turning, if you wanted to put a positive spin on it. Once the pale sun finally peeped through the tent flap, she sat up irritably and rubbed her burning eyes with the heels of her itchy, icicle hands. She hadn't been able to shake the bone-deep cold from her limbs all night, especially after the fire burned out.

How Fox had happily snored all night long, Tennie had no idea.

But as the morning sun woke the trees, they blazed around her in a celebration of shimmering, variegated color. *Good morning, Tennessee.*

The light thawed her face and soul. "Good mornin' your-self," she whispered to the woods, sighing in contentment.

"Tennie, whoa."

Tennie twisted to see Fox staring wide-eyed with a finger lifted.

"Don't say 'whoa,'" Tennie muttered, hoping Fox hadn't heard her talking to the trees. "Every time you say 'whoa,' something awful happens."

"It's just . . . your sweatshirt."

"What about it?"

"The back. It's covered in mud."

"What?" Tennie twisted to see the back of her sweatshirt.

Wobbly lines of dried mud were smeared across the lovely fabric. The temper Tennie'd been famous for when she was little flared, sending angry bubbles to the surface. "What the heck, Fox? Is this a joke? Cause it *ain't* funny. This was a good shirt!"

"It wasn't me; swear on my abuela's grave." Fox's eyes were amber saucers.

Tennie felt sick. She stretched the loose jersey out to study the mess. The muddy slashes and curves almost looked like . . .

"Is that writing?" A sickening weight settled in Tennie's chest. The shape of a D was up at the top, plain as day. Words, written in mud, scrawled across the back of her shirt. Tennie's head swam trying to read them upside down.

"If you hold still, I'll try and read it," Fox said, resting their hands gently on Tennie's shoulders. The corners of their mouth tugged downward in concentration—or worry.

Tennie tried to keep still but couldn't. She needed the muddy writing off her body like you'd need a spider off your neck—right then, not later.

"I need to change," she mumbled, pulling away and stumbling toward the Sanchez-Griffins' house. Fox followed, and the two of them managed to make it up the stairs to Fox's room without Fox's parents noticing.

"I'll find you a new shirt," Fox reassured Tennie, digging through their drawers. "Either of these work?"

Tennie tried to keep calm, shaking her head. "Won't fit. You're a string bean."

Fox rummaged and came up with a giant fuzzy black sweater. Tennie changed in the bathroom, then came back holding the dirty sweatshirt away from her body. They spread it across Fox's carpet and studied the red-brown words.

Ded forrst.

"Whoa."

"Fox," Tennie said shakily, "if you say that one more time . . ."

"Okay. What the *heck*? And more important, *who*?"

Tennie pulled her hands into the soft, fuzzy sleeves of Fox's sweater, suspicion itching her mind. "I was so cold last night,

Fox. *Ghost*-cold. It started freezing right before you drew that forest on my back. I couldn't get warm, just like after the marbles. And the watch."

"Tennie—"

"What?"

"I didn't draw a forest on your back last night."

"That ain't funny, Fox."

Fox looked hurt, shuddering. "I'm not joking, Tennie. I didn't draw a forest."

"Well, you just don't remember. You were sleepy, s'all. I guessed mountains, an' you said no, then I guessed houses, an'—"

Fox shook their head grimly. Tennie's mind raced to fill in the blanks.

"Okay. So it was a ghost. I was talking to one of the ghosts. *Neat.* That is just super, super *neat*, Fox. Double neat topped with . . . so much more *neat*!" Tennie paced across the carpet, shivering. A giggle escaped her, then grew into a bubbling, zany laugh she couldn't put a stop to. She sank cross-legged to the carpet.

"Tennie, you're weirding me out."

Tennie gasped between guffaws, clutching her sides. She felt the rhythm of the shuddering sobs before the tears hit her eyes. She hadn't done her whole overwhelmed-laughter-turned-sob-fest routine in at least four years—definitely not since she'd started wearing gloves.

"Tennie?" Fox's voice was worried. "Are you okay?"

"I'm fine," Tennie choked.

"No offense? But I don't believe you."

"It's just . . . the ghost *touched* me." Tennie shuddered. "We *talked*! Without you helping me hear it. I hate ghosts talking to me if you're not there, too." Her face crumpled again. *And now, I'm crying in front of Fox.* That wasn't a thing sturdy, mature Lancasters did. Tennie was going to die of embarrassment.

"I've only helped, like, two people see ghosts before, but they've never had that trouble. But since you can release them . . . maybe normal rules don't apply. This is uncharted territory." Fox raked a hand through their hair, looking nervous.

"Well, that's just fine, ain't it?" Tennie sniffed. "I reckon I make a real cute guinea pig. All I need is a box full of Timothy hay, a water bottle, and an emotional support hamster so I don't have a heart attack next time a ghost decides to use me for *a dry-erase board*!"

Fox fidgeted with their hoodie strings. "You'll get used to it. The first time I saw a ghost in a parking lot, I dropped a whole carton of eggs, right there on the asphalt—*splat*! They scared me to death. At least they did until—" Fox broke off, lips tightening.

"Until what?" Tennie said, sniffing.

"Forget it. Anyway, the point is? Everybody's scared of something." Fox's eyes flitted to the box of maybe-haunted things, then back to Tennie's face.

Mrs. Sanchez-Griffin's voice called up the stairs. *"Did I hear y'all sneak in? There's leftover pizza and hot chocolate down here!"*

Tennie scrubbed a sleeve across her swollen eyes. "Guess we should go down. Don't want to make trouble for y'all."

"Nah, it's okay! Mom's chill. We can wait a minute until . . ." Fox gestured vaguely at Tennie's blotchy face.

Tennie struggled to slow her breathing. Fox gave her a side hug, and Tennie let her head droop to their shoulder. "So what *does* scare you, if ghosts don't do it anymore?"

A cloud passed over Fox's face. "Not finding any ghosts, I guess."

"You're *somethin'*," Tennie muttered.

"No, think about it," Fox insisted. "No ghosts means there's nothing . . . more. Nothing extra. Or *after*."

"So, it's endings, then," Tennie guessed. "That's your scary thing."

"I guess. Doesn't that bother *you*?"

Tennie twisted her face, considering her words carefully.

She thought about the sweet calm of Poppy's walking stick. "I guess not. I reckon folks leave traces of themselves around, good or bad. Their love. The things they care about. Nothing ever really leaves." Tennie glanced at her ruined sweatshirt and scowled. "Kind of like *stains*."

"Leave that to my Pa," Fox reassured her. "That man is a laundry sorcerer. Once, I saw him remove a whole lasagna from a pair of socks."

Tennie rolled her eyes and giggled. "Dork."

"Here, I'll put it in the hamper, and bring it back to you tomorrow!"

"Let's take a picture of it first, though," Tennie said suddenly, digging out her phone.

"Why?"

"I dunno." Tennie gazed down at the muddy words, with their wobbly mix of capital and lowercase letters, like a young kid had written it. Something nagged her. Tennie's memory kept rewinding to Harper learning to write in kindergarten. It had come easy to Shi, but Harper's first attempts resembled the muddy scrawl, and had taken a lot of effort. "Seems like a lot of trouble for a ghost to go to, is all. Don't they usually just . . . float around?"

"I guess. They sort of go in repeating loops, like a GIF. They relive the same thing over and over a lot."

"So, don't it strike you odd that this one didn't? It answered my questions. It was playing our back-scratching game, Fox." Tennie snapped a photo of the muddy sweatshirt with her cell phone. "That ain't bein' stuck in a GIF."

"Who knows why ghosts do what they do? It doesn't *mean* anything. C'mon, you'll feel better once we eat."

Tennie followed Fox to the kitchen. Together, they nuked pizza and poured hot chocolate into mugs from the saucepan Mrs. Sanchez-Griffin had left on the stove. Soon after, soft rain *tinged* against the kitchen window, so while Tennie dawdled over her food, Fox sprinted out to rescue their camping gear.

Through the watery glass, Tennie watched old trees swaying as the hissing wind snatched their leaves and sent them fluttering into the yard.

Dead forest, the ghost had written. The words felt like a twisting knife.

Those were Poppy's woods. They were *her* woods—hers and Fox's. Their canopy was a magic world where Tennie felt free. The trees' roots cut through layers and layers of the earth's memory—they needed peace to flourish. Tennie and the forest were cut from the same cloth.

"You aren't dangerous," Tennie whispered softly to the trees. "I don't believe that for a minute."

After Fox clattered through the front door with their gear, the two put on rain slickers and tromped off down the dirt road to walk Tennie home to Mimsy's. *I should be scared right now*, Tennie thought. But Fox was with her, and they were walking down the road in broad daylight.

As they laughed and joked, the wind grew stronger, attacking their backs in wild gusts. The whistling around the branches gradually deepened into a slow, hollow howl. Fox reached for Tennie's hand, their fingers tightening around hers. Electricity tingled down Tennie's neck.

The two of them turned around slowly to sense—but not quite see—a ravenous, empty, nothing-place just behind them on the road. Tennie's stomach was an elevator, free-falling to the basement. The watch ghost had found them.

"Empty . . ." The spirit hissed and howled. Its death-rattle words clamped around Tennie's middle like an iron chain, pulling her down, down, down into despair. *"Empty and dead!"*

Fox took a "don't mess with us" stance. "Get lost, dillweed!" they yelled. Tennie froze, waiting for the ghost to go. But if anything, the wind grew angrier. A heavy, invisible something landed between her and Fox and scratched a long, fast line into the red dirt down the length of the road.

"Let's go," Fox yelped. They clasped cold hands and ran.

Tennie tried to keep up, but her feet were heavy as lead. It was like one of those horrible dreams about running through water. The sadness at her heels kept pulling and pulling on her, like a lonely vacuum.

"Tennie, c'mon!" Fox pleaded. "Hurry!"

Tennie tried. Out of the corner of her eye, *the trees looked twisted and dead.* But when she looked to the side, they were alive and well again. "What are you doing?" yelled Fox. "Don't look back!"

Rotted gray forest whirred just outside her line of vision, shriveled and broken and desiccated. Her eyes blurred with stinging tears as the cold wind whipped across her. *Don't look,* she warned herself.

Tennie thought she saw other dead things, too—white animal bones, shattered trees, and rocky ground stripped of black soil. The mountain was scraped flat, its heart exposed and bleeding crimson.

But every sideways glance told her this was wrong—the woods were still lush with life. The watch ghost was slithering into her head, distorting her mind. Tennie clutched Fox's hand tighter and squeezed her eyes shut, letting her footfalls match her friend's as she ran blind the rest of the way to Mimsy's.

CHAPTER 10

When they charged into Mimsy's
yard breathless, Tennie was appalled to find Mimsy's wraparound porch peppered with a small congregation of people. A
red-haired woman in a khaki uniform, who was accompanied
by a teenage boy in glasses, clutched a white bundle in her
arms. A forest ranger, Tennie realized, seeing the state park's
logo on the Jeep in the driveway. The ranger and an apron-clad
Mimsy chatted while Mr. Bolton stood off to the side in a pink
polo shirt, nodding sagely and humming in agreement.

Tennie paused to catch her breath.

"Your face is white," Fox whispered. "You okay?"

Tennie's lungs burned. She couldn't yet put words to what

she'd just seen in the woods—the dead trees, the broken mountain, the bones. "Dead forest," she managed between gulps of air.

"Here, hold still," Fox frowned, untangling a twig from Tennie's hair. "What do you mean, 'dead forest'?"

Mimsy caught sight of Tennie and waved.

"Tell you . . . later," Tennie huffed, trying to make herself look calm.

Fox stared at the porch for a second, swallowed hard, then began backing away. "I, uh, I'd better head home now . . ."

Tennie gasped and put her hands to her hips. "You are *not* goin' back in those woods. You're comin' with me, an' you can spend the night. Mimsy'll drive you home tomorrow."

"I dunno . . ."

"Well, *I* know. I saw something out there. It isn't safe. Now, c'mon."

Tennie tried to act normal as they passed the row of cars in the driveway—the Jeep, Mimsy's Buick, and a familiar sleek car with tinted windows. Fox's fists knotted at their sides. "That's the car that almost ran us down yesterday!" Fox growled.

"CAW, CAW!" French Fry swooped across the yard and landed on the fancy car, donating a stream of droppings to the windshield. "Good girl, French Fry," Fox muttered.

"Shoo, little bird, fly away, now!" Mr. Bolton called from the porch, waving his arms at the crow. French Fry cocked her head and regarded him coolly before flying off.

Mr. Bolton was *the terrible driver,* Tennie realized in a tiny flash of anger. *Prob'ly ain't used to driving the back roads in the Hollow.*

As they climbed the porch steps, Tennie saw inside the park ranger's bundle—it was one of the crows from French Fry's murder. Fox gave a soft gasp and ran over to inspect it.

"My, my, my," Mimsy murmured, worrying her hands together. "Poor little creature."

The ranger gave them a friendly smile. "Hey there, Fox. Think this little fella's got himself a broken foot," she said in a soft mountain twang.

Fox's chin trembled. "He's one of the babies from French Fry's clutch last year. How bad is it, Honey?"

It took Tennie a moment to realize the ranger's *name* was Honey. The woman shook her head, ponytail swishing. "Not that bad, punkin. I'll probably turn him loose and see if his flock takes care of him. Crows do that, sometimes."

The black bird in the towel seemed resigned to the blanket, twisting its head curiously. The ranger chuckled, clucking her tongue softly. *Mama'd like bein' friends with her,* Tennie thought.

Honey reminded her of Mama in a way—calm and happy when she was helping folks, like Mama was as a first responder.

"I can't for the life of me figure out how he managed to hurt it," Honey finished, gently unwrapping the crow and setting it free. "It's just one toe, but it's a pretty nasty break."

The crow flapped to the ground, hobbling, and its family swooped down to join it. Mimsy tossed them half a banana from a red plastic cup, and French Fry snatched it expertly, bringing it to her injured son.

"There, see? He's got good family," Honey said. "Mind if I wash my hands in your sink, Ilene?"

"Not a'tall. And let me fix you a jar of sweet tea for the road," Mimsy fussed, and the adults shuffled inside.

Tennie was suddenly—painfully—aware of the strange boy still standing on Mimsy's porch. Her palms went sweaty from stranger-nerves. She jabbed Fox in the leg with the toe of her shoe and shyly tilted her head, waiting to be introduced.

Fox stared at their shoes, a stupid, sheepish grin plastered to their face. The freckle-faced boy sighed, giving Tennie a look of empathy.

"Honey's my mom. I'm Tyler," he said, extending a hand. "Fox's best friend."

Fox's best friend. "Nice to meet you," Tennie blurted,

giving him the world's quickest fist bump. She squelched a flare of jealousy. "I'm Tennessee Lancaster. I'm just visiting my grandma."

"Hey, Fox."

"Hey, buddy, long time no see," Fox managed, ears red. "I've been meaning to come by . . ."

Tyler gave Fox a pointed look. "Oh, you mean like for my *birthday party*? There was paintball and everything!" He rolled up a sleeve to show off a bruise. "My cousin's deadly."

"You know me. I'd forget my head if it wasn't screwed on," Fox muttered, sheepish.

"I know, buddy. I'm surprised you didn't bring over an apology cookie like you did last year when you missed it! And the year before that, come to think of it."

"Wait, an apology cookie?" Tennie asked, glancing at Fox.

"It's practically a tradition now!" Tyler said, smiling so hard his eyes disappeared. "They bake a big-booty chocolate chip cookie with something written on it in candy. Last year, it was, 'Oops!' and the year before was 'U R 11! Yay puberty!'"

"Shut *up*, Tyler," Fox growled, face flushing.

Tennie's mind zoomed to the cookie—the one she'd thought Fox made to welcome her to the Hollow—and her stomach wrung itself like a washrag. That had been meant for *Tyler*.

"I bet the next one will be short and sweet. Something like 'Friends' with a question mark," Tennie said dryly, trying to seem less hurt than she was. Fox groaned miserably and muttered under their breath.

"Aww, don't sweat it," Tyler said, pulling Fox into a side hug. "You've probably been too busy showin' Tennessee around the Hollow to bake."

"I've got your present at my house, though," Fox argued. "I just haven't had time to wrap it yet. I'll bring it by tomorrow!"

"Cool! I'm doin' a Zelda marathon with my friends Katy and Caleb then, if y'all want to hang out." Honey stepped out on the porch, jangling her Jeep keys and waving bye to Mimsy and Mr. Bolton.

Tyler grinned. "Nice to meet you, Tennessee!" Then, on the porch steps, he paused next to Fox, touching their elbow and whispering something into their ear. Tennie frowned and shifted her weight as the two did an elaborate handshake ritual.

What's so juicy that he can't say it out loud? Tennie wondered. *Secrets, secrets are no fun . . .*

She knew it was immature to feel jealous. Fox had a life in the Hollow—including friends—and Tennie was the outsider. But for the past two days, she'd pretended the world was nothing but her and Fox, inside the old-growth forest with its ghosts.

Of course, that was a silly fantasy. But for some reason, that truth burned all the way down like bad cold medicine.

When Tennie added in the fact that Fox had lied about that silly cookie, it was a recipe for a foul mood. She yanked open her duffle and retrieved Poppy's old wool gloves. "You hungry?" Tennie asked Fox sharply.

Fox nodded, not meeting Tennie's eyes.

The two of them went inside, hurrying through the living room where Mimsy and Mr. Bolton sat chatting. In the kitchen, Tennie yanked the bread from the cabinet and slathered mayonnaise and mustard onto the pieces—a little harder than necessary.

Ever since Tennie had outgrown pitching hissy fits, she'd developed the perplexing habit of swinging in the opposite direction. Now, she'd act polite as peas, but formal and stiff, too, like a vaguely annoyed dental hygienist. No matter how hard she tried, she couldn't find the exit from her bad mood. Fox tried to joke a few times, and Tennie snipped each attempt into tiny pieces with her short replies.

"If you were a shape-shifter," Fox tried again, "and you turned into a chicken, then you ate a box of nuggets . . .would that make you a cannibal?"

"No. I don't s'pose so."

Fox leaned against the counter. "Why not?"

"If you were still a human at heart, it's not cannibalism. And if you had a chicken's soul, you wouldn't care about bein' a cannibal. You wouldn't have a *conscience*."

Fox's mouth twisted. They ran a hand over their curls nervously. "Tennie, are you mad at me?"

"Why would I be mad?"

"Your *eyes* say you're mad at me."

"D-don't put words in my eyes," Tennie stammered. "Anyway, I'm not mad. I hardly ever get mad."

"Everybody gets mad," Fox countered, folding a piece of bologna in half nervously. "Trust me. I oughta know."

"What's that s'posed to mean?"

Fox's eyes darted around the floor. "My brain's impulsive. And I forget a lot of important stuff, especially when I'm excited. And sometimes, the more important a thing is, the harder it gets to follow through. It's just how I'm wired up. And trust me—folks get mad."

Tennie's grip on the butter knife loosened. "So?"

"So, it makes me afraid to disappoint people. I don't ever want to do it on purpose, and sometimes . . . I go overboard." Fox looked like they'd just swallowed a chip sideways.

Tennie swiped a stray drop of mustard with a paper towel.

"You mean, like if someone new thought you'd made them a welcome present . . ."

Fox looked sheepish. "It's hard for me to say, 'Hey, paws off, cute girl—that ain't for you!' Because I didn't want to disappoint you. And I wish I *had* thought of bringing you a welcome present."

"I guess I can understand not wanting to upset folks," Tennie said softly, pretending not to notice she'd just been called cute. Her stomach fluttered with butterflies.

"Anyway. Sorry."

"S'okay."

"Speaking of upsetting folks," Fox whispered, waving a piece of bologna toward the living room, "you might not like this? But I don't trust Mister Vehicular Homicide in there."

"Mr. Bolton? Why?"

"Are you kidding me? He almost ran us down like possums! French Fry doesn't like him. Besides, Tyler told me he gives him a bad feeling."

"Oh. Well. If *Tyler* says so . . ."

"He's a pretty good judge of character."

Mimsy's chuckling voice drifted through the doorway. Mimsy, who'd been bravely hiding her money troubles from the family while living alone since Poppy passed. Tennie's grandmother sounded happy, and Tennie's hackles raised in her defense. "I'm sure it's hard for Mr. Bolton, being an outsider. Y'all have been close-knit in this Hollow all your life. Folks just don't like strangers."

"You're not from here, and I like you a lot," Fox observed with a lopsided smile.

Tennie blushed. But still, she didn't feel right about the two of them runnin' Mimsy's beau down, right here in Mimsy's kitchen.

"Let's talk about something else."

"Okay. Why'd you say 'dead forest' when we got here?"

Tennie dropped her voice. "I told you. I saw things in the woods."

"Ghosts?"

Tennie shook her head, then pulled Fox through the kitchen door onto the back porch for privacy.

"While we were running from the watch ghost, I kept seeing these flashes out of the corner of my eye. Pictures of the forest gone bad, like expired milk. The trees were all wrong, and the air smelled like rot." She tossed the rest of her sandwich to the crows, her stomach too sour to eat. "*Dead forest*, Fox. Just like the writing on my shirt."

"But the marble ghosts wrote that, not the watch ghost," Fox pointed out.

"Exactly," Tennie said. "Don't it seem uncanny? They sent me the same message."

Fox grinned. "You think the ghosts are cheating off each other's homework?"

"Don't laugh, Fox! They feel . . . connected, somehow," Tennie insisted. "Isn't that how it works? Ghosts go restless because of unresolved secrets? Maybe we're supposed to figure it out and help."

Fox raised an eyebrow. "Or we could just keep huntin' for new ghosts and have fun. And not overthink it."

Tennie was terrified to go into her beloved forest again with these particular ghosts still on the loose. But simply staying out forever was unthinkable.

"What if we could put them to rest? Help them *move on*."

Fox's face shuttered and they crossed their wiry arms across their chest. "I dunno, Tennie."

"Why not?" Tennie demanded. "If this is the only way to put things back to normal, we have to try!"

Fox scoffed. "What part of ghost hunting seems normal to you? Wasn't spooky the *point*?"

The point was being in the forest with you! Tennie wanted to yell. But she couldn't just *tell* Fox that. And now, it wasn't even safe to go in the forest by herself.

"Just . . . promise me you'll think about it, at least?" she asked. Tennie didn't love how pitiful her voice sounded.

Fox sighed. "Alright. I'll think about it. But I should probably go home for a while. I've been slacking on my chores, and I don't want to end up grounded."

"Okay," Tennie mumbled, trailing after Fox around the wraparound porch. "You sure you don't at least want a ride home?"

Fox waved her off. "I'll be okay."

"But the watch ghost!" Tennie protested. "Fox, don't you think it's dangerous to run off through the forest alone, after what I saw today?"

Tennie thought she saw Fox give a tiny eye roll. "No offense, Tennie? But I've been dealing with ghosts a lot longer than you."

Soft thunder rumbled across the mountains, and the woods loomed deep and dark. "These ghosts wouldn't be loose in the first place without my help," Tennie argued, panicking. "And if something happens to you, I'd be to blame! At least let me walk with you."

"Again, no offense? But I can probably run faster if you're not with me," Fox said, waving apologetically. They headed down the driveway and didn't look back.

"What in the heck just happened?" Tennie whispered to herself. She swallowed the hard lump in her throat as the trees swallowed Fox whole, leaving Tennie all alone.

CHAPTER 11

That evening, Mimsy tried to lift

her granddaughter's funk by insisting that she, Tennie, and Mr. Bolton all go down to the fried catfish place for dinner.

Tennie managed to beg out of the excursion. She wasn't eager to sit in on a night of elderly flirting, so instead she stayed home and moped in her bedroom. Fox's weird mood swing earlier had left Tennie feeling raw and out of sorts. Her mind kept replaying their conversation over and over, trying to find where it had gone sideways, and blaming herself even though she didn't know what she'd done wrong.

"This is dumb," she said aloud when she'd run out of tears. "All I wanted three days ago was some peace and quiet and *space*. And now I have this whole house TO MYSELF!" she hollered, smiling down the dark hallway.

It occurred to her that she was completely alone, with not a soul around except through the dark woods, upstairs in a dark house. And Mimsy, whose house was out in the sticks even by Howler's Hollow standards, rarely locked any of her doors. That wouldn't do.

Tennie took Poppy's walking stick in one hand and her cell phone in the other, then systematically flipped on every upstairs light in the house—the hallway, the bathroom, the other guest bedroom with Poppy's old paintings in it, and Mimsy's room. Then she crept back down the stairs in her socks and locked the front door. As she did, she hummed Poppy's song in time with her thumping heart.

Flip, flip, flip! She turned on the switches to all the downstairs lights, saving the kitchen for last, where she locked the back door, too.

Satisfied that the house was secure, Tennie rummaged through the fridge for some leftover biscuits and jam, then settled at the table to check her text messages.

There was a quick "I love you and miss you so much, Spooky Bear!" from her mom, a drawing of a snake in a cowboy hat saying "Ssssee you soon!" from her dad, and one text from her older brother that just said: "Call me."

Tennie reluctantly pressed the call button by her brother's number. He answered after the first ring: "What took you so long?"

"Nice to hear from you, too, Birch," Tennie said through a mouthful of biscuit.

"Sorry. That was rude of me, Tenn. I'm tryin' to do better about that."

Tennie nearly choked. "Since when do you have manners?"

"Since . . . Mom and Dad made me go talk to someone. A counselor dude who wears PAC-MAN bow ties."

Tennie furrowed her brow. "Why?"

Birch sighed heavily into the phone, hurting Tennie's ear, then stayed quiet for a long minute. "'Cause I'm a little depressed, I guess."

Tennie clutched the phone. She'd only been gone from her family for three days, and now Birch had gotten blue, too, before Mama even got started up again. "Why? 'Cause we moved?"

"Naw. I've been like this for a while, I guess. Anyway, I'm s'posed to be working on not masking it with anger." He said the last words in a funny voice, and Tennie couldn't tell if he was being sarcastic or not. But either way, these were the most honest words she'd heard Birch say in a year. She swallowed hard, not wanting to ruin it.

"Is that why you wanted me to call?"

"No. Tennie, don't get upset, but . . . I think Mom's expectin' another baby."

"What??" Tennie's pulse doubled. Of all the things Birch could have said, that was possibly the worst. "Why do you think that?"

"She's yarfing every morning and sleeping in longer than me. And I found a test in the garbage can," Birch said, his voice dropping to a hush. On her brother's end of the phone, Tennie heard a door open, then a chorus of crickets—he'd gone outside so their parents wouldn't hear him. "And that's not all, Tenn."

It was weird, Birch being the one who knew all the family's secrets. Tennie felt frantic, like things at home were speeding toward disaster. "Spit it out."

"Dad's new job fell through. He hasn't told us yet, but this house is flimsy as paper—you hear everything through the walls. The company owner got into some trouble, and I think they're layin' a bunch of people off. Mom's planning to start workin' soon, but . . ."

Tennie's mouth went dry. "She can only be an EMT for a while, if there's a baby coming. That's bad."

"Yep. We're broke from moving already, an' Mom's way too proud to ask Mimsy for help. You know how the two of them are."

Tennie did know. *And anyway, Mimsy's broke, too,* Tennie thought, not that Mimsy would ever admit it. Mr. Bolton, on the other hand, had vacation condos scattered from here to Maui. Maybe he could help somehow.

"I've got something to tell you, too. Mimsy's seein' someone. Romantically."

"Gross, Tennie! I didn't need to know that!"

"Listen, Birch! He's rich as butter on bacon. Really stable, and really into Mimsy."

"Okay," Birch's voice drawled. "I'm starting to see your point, but you know as well as I do Mom would rather drink hot dog water than ask anybody for a favor. Especially anyone connected to Mimsy. Mom always worries Mimsy thinks her . . . you know, depression, is a burden, like Poppy's was."

"What? Birch, Poppy was never blue," Tennie said, tensing. "He just hiked and worked more than Mimsy liked sometimes."

A long sigh came through the receiver. "Every fall, like clockwork, yeah. Let's not argue about this, okay? We got plenty to worry about already."

Tennie swallowed a worried prickle in her throat. "We'll just have to think of something."

There was a gentle rapping at the front door. Tennie peeked through the blinds but didn't see Mr. Bolton's car. He and Mimsy were still gone. "I gotta go, Birch." She picked up Poppy's walking stick, stalked to the front door, and peered through the peephole. No one was there. The knock came again, and she jumped, heart pounding.

"Tennie?" came a muffled voice.

Was that Fox, out so late? Tennie unlocked and opened the inside door, peering through the outside screen. It rained softly outside, and water giggled its way down the porch gutters. But the porch was empty—no Fox. Tennie pressed her lips together, fingers tightening on the handle. Then, she spotted it: her neatly folded sweatshirt resting on the gently swaying porch swing. Atop it was a bundle of soggy goldenrod stalks tied up with a long piece of grass in a haphazard bow. There was a white slip of paper nestled beneath it.

In shockingly neat cursive, the rust-colored ink read: *Sorry for earlier. Glad the stains came out. It's such a pretty color on you. Friends?*

Tennie pressed her lips together in a smile. "Dingus," she

whispered. After a quick examination of her sweatshirt, she discovered it was good as new. Mr. Sanchez-Griffin *was* a stain genius. She nuzzled her face into the soft fabric and turned to hurry back inside.

Her sock-clad feet paused on the smooth boards of the porch. Something felt . . . off. *It's too quiet*, she realized, noticing that the soothing gurgle of the gutters had fallen silent. Tennie's eyebrows knitted as she scanned the dark yard. If anything, the pittering rain came down harder than ever, making the grass glisten in the porch light. Tennie craned her neck up at the gutter in confusion. *What the heck?*

Cold from the floorboards bit through her socks, chilling her feet to the bones. Tennie's ears tingled, and she began to shiver. Then, slowly, she understood that the noise had stopped because rain had frozen solid inside the gutters. Her breath rose in clouds.

Ghosts.

"Fox," Tennie said in a strangled whimper, reaching for her friend's hand instinctively even though Fox wasn't there. What her fingers caught instead was a hand too small to be Fox's and much too cold. Tennie glanced down to see the hand was *not really there.*

She shrieked at the emptiness, and her socks slipped on

the smooth boards as she tried to run back into the house. She fell hard, knocking the wind out of herself. For a few seconds, she lay splayed out flat on her back, gasping for freezing air, unable to move.

Light footsteps began at the back of the wraparound porch, then skipped around either side of the house. *Ta-THUMP, ta-THUMP, ta-THUMP.* Whoever they were giggled and hummed softly in voices that sounded so much like Shiloh and Harper's—but absolutely weren't Tennie's sisters. Tennie recognized the tune. It was the old campfire song she'd been singing earlier. *What will the waves wash up next?*

Tennie choked and struggled to her feet. Shaking, she tried to open the screen door, but it held fast. *Locked.* With a terrified sob, she yanked hard on the handle over and over, eyes fixed on the nearest corner of the house. The porch lights flickered treacherously, threatening to go out.

"It'll wash up green bones, and they'll follow you home!" a breathy voice called. The skipping steps grew close enough for Tennie's feet to feel vibrations in the boards. *Ta-thump, ta-thump, ta-squelch, squelch, squelch.*

"C'mon, *open*," Tennie gasped, giving the screen door handle one final, desperate jerk. It held fast.

Tennie's heart scaled her throat. Around the corner of the

porch, small, muddy footprints appeared. *Squelch, squelch, squelch.* They crept toward Tennie, slipping and smearing across Mimsy's clean floorboards.

Tennie reached behind her and tried to dig her nails through the outer door's screen. If she managed to rip a big enough hole, she could open the wooden inner door and squirm inside the house.

"Sister," a singsong voice echoed faintly from the direction of the footprints, *"where are youuuu?"*

"I'm here," whispered another voice just beside Tennie's ear. Tennie froze, too terrified to move. She shut her eyes tight and waited for something awful to happen. Blood whooshed in her ears for what felt like an eternity.

Footfalls danced around her, then trailed away. Tennie forced her eyes open. She scratched at the screen door in determination, and finally her fingernails found a tiny hole that gave way with a satisfying *rrrrrrrrip.* Grabbing the inner door handle, she twisted and shoved it open. Just as she started toward the hole in the screen, a horrible scream came from the back porch, sending echoes into the night. A deep rumble shook the whole house, rattling the windowpanes.

Tennie stood transfixed as up through the cracks of the wooden floorboards oozed wet, red mud, flowing across the porch and cascading into the flower beds below in thick, spattering piles. She yelped as the mud seeped through her socks, and she fought to scramble headfirst through the ripped screen door and into the house.

Just when she thought her heart might stop, the peaceful gurgle of the gutters started up again. Tennie glanced over her shoulder. The porch sprawled in its usual modest way, clean as a whistle. Nothing was amiss except the hole and her sweatshirt, which lay rumpled atop scattered yellow flowers beside the door.

It was as if nothing had happened.

Just then, headlight beams eased up the gravel driveway, slow and smooth. Mr. Bolton had brought Mimsy home.

Tennie disentangled herself from the shredded screen door, still shaking like a leaf. Mimsy got out of the car, pocketbook tucked under her arm. She stared in bewilderment at her granddaughter and the mangled door. "Well, Storybook, what happened here?" Mr. Bolton hovered behind Mimsy, frowning in disapproval.

"I—I got locked out," Tennie stammered.

"Back in my day, if you broke a person's door, you'd either pay for it in chores or a whippin'," Mr. Bolton observed, raising a disapproving eyebrow.

"There'll be no need for that now," Mimsy said firmly, unlocking the screen door. "I'm sorry you locked yourself out, Darlin'. I reckon you done it by habit, didn't you? But you don't have to worry about prowlers in the Hollow. Just for giggles, though, I reckon I'll get you a copy of the house key tomorrow."

Tennie couldn't look her grandmother in the face. "I'm so sorry I broke it, Mimsy."

Mimsy patted Tennie's arm firmly. "That ol' screen needed replacing anyway. It was startin' to let the pests in."

Tennie walked numbly into the house. Mr. Bolton harrumphed and hung around in the kitchen, while Mimsy made coffee and insisted he spend the night in the big downstairs guest room. Tennie retreated to her room, cradling her sweatshirt. For a while, she sat on her bed, stunned. She clutched Poppy's walking stick. Its peacefulness gradually washed away the terror of what she'd just been through, along with the mortification of Mimsy thinking Tennie'd shredded the screen door like a badly behaved cat—just because she'd locked herself out of the house.

"We gotta put an end to this nonsense," Tennie muttered.

She grabbed her phone and texted Fox.

Thx for your note. We need 2 talk. Ghost stuff!!

Tennie brushed Fox's note idly against her face, waiting ten, fifteen, twenty minutes for a text reply that didn't come. The note was strangely soft, like thistledown. Curious, Tennie held it to the light to study it—and noticed faint words on its back side.

She flipped it over.

On the back, in wobbly, rust-colored scrawl were the words *its happuning agin. ded forrst.*

Tennie gasped and dropped the paper to the pumpkin print bedspread, heart in her throat. The writing matched her sweatshirt's, only there was more to the message this time. In her gut Tennie felt—*she knew*—that the ruined forest the watch ghost had shown her wasn't some freaky coincidence. Tennie reached for her cell phone with shaky hands, opened the camera app, and snapped a picture. Then, with wobbly thumbs, she texted the photo to Fox.

She waited, her breathing ragged with excitement.

Several seconds later, Fox responded.

It's late. Thanks for the photo of a blanket, I guess??

Tennie's cheeks burned—she couldn't tell if it was from annoyance or embarrassment—and she scrolled up to the photo she'd just sent.

It was like Fox said: a photo of her bedspread. There was no paper. "What the heck?" Tennie whispered. She reached beside her for the paper, but her hand came up empty. Tennie threw back the throw pillows and blankets. When she didn't find the note there, she dangled off the side of the bed to check beneath it, in case it had fallen. It was gone.

"But . . ." Tennie scrolled through the photos again, for good measure. There was an artsy shot of her hot chocolate that morning, and another she'd sneaked of Fox dancing in front of the microwave. Finally, she saw the photo of her sweatshirt spread out on Fox's bedroom floor.

But in the photo, her shirt was spotless. Mud free. No "dead forest" message.

Tennie flopped back onto the messy pile of pillows, head spinning. "It was there," she whispered. "I know it was." But she didn't have a lick of proof, and it sounded bonkers to claim a piece of paper had up and vanished. *I'll just show Fox the picture of the clean sweatshirt tomorrow*, she thought. Then they'd understand, and the two of them could figure this out together.

They would find a way to soothe the ghosts, and with any luck, Tennie could talk Fox out of ghost hunting for a while. They could play cards and build fires and eat cookies, like normal people.

Then, she'd focus on a way to help her family get settled with everybody's pride still intact, before Mama had any trouble with the blues or her new pregnancy.

"There's nothing I can do about it tonight," Tennie whispered. "Tomorrow."

She curled up on top of Mimsy's throw pillows and waited to be so worn out, sleep would overtake her jumpiness.

When it finally did, she slept with the lights on.

CHAPTER 12

It stopped raining late the next morning, leaving the world a mirrored mess of puddles and sky. Groggy and grumpy, Tennie yanked on a thick wool sweater and made a beeline for the back garden—the spot in Mimsy's yard where the sun hit hardest.

She ached with loneliness, and noisy thoughts chased each other around her head like gravel in a blender. For a while, she paced circles around the pumpkin patch, waiting and staring hungrily at the forest. She wanted to whisper her mixed-up secrets to the trees. But she wasn't about to wander in there alone. Not while it was haunted. Not while things were bent on following her *home*.

Finally, she decided it wasn't too early to text Fox.

GHOST STUFF, SOS!!

Tennie plopped down on a giant pumpkin and waited for a reply, shivering. She hadn't been able to get warm ever since the marble ghosts had visited last night. French Fry hopped around the garden with her injured son, and Tennie tossed them pieces of the muffin she was too anxious to eat. Finally, her phone buzzed with a text from Fox.

Can't meet now.
Chores at the restaurant

Tennie scowled and growled under her breath. How long would that take? She didn't love the idea of going another round with the ghosts before she talked to Fox again.

"I see you came out for some fresh air, Tennessee."

Tennie nearly jumped out of her skin. She whipped around to see Mr. Bolton. He wore an oatmeal-colored dress jacket and shiny shoes. *He always looks ready to go to church. Or sell a fancy car*, Tennie noticed, giving him an awkward wave.

"Mornin', Mr. Bolton."

"Nice little garden your granny's got here," he observed. French Fry squawked at him, then flew off, clearly having met her tolerance threshold for human company.

"*Mimsy's* got the nicest pumpkins in the county," Tennie agreed. She ground her teeth, not in the mood.

Mr. Bolton chuckled. "That doesn't surprise me in a place like this. The mountain's rich in resource."

That's an odd way to describe a place, Tennie thought. If someone said, "My, what a lovely sister you have, Mr. Smith. She seems rich in resource," they'd be treated to two black eyes and a ticket out of town. In Tennie's mind, mountains and people were the same that way—they just *were*. "I like it here just fine," Tennie said politely. "It's something pretty special."

"Indeed, it is. Did you know these mountains are among the oldest in the world? They predate the dinosaurs."

Tennie *did* know that already, but she forced a charitable look. "That's somethin'." She wanted to add, *now go away*, but held her tongue. She had enough worry without stirring up bad blood with Mimsy's new beau.

Mr. Bolton put his hands on his hips and kept right on lecturing. "The simple-hearted folks in these parts have lived here for centuries without understanding the blessing they have right at their doorstep."

Tennie's face went persimmon sour, and she rolled her eyes so hard she saw stars. "I don't mean any disrespect, Mr. Bolton, but have you *met* folks from Howler's Hollow? They can't go a whole season without throwin' some kind of festival to celebrate this place. They appreciate the blessing of it."

Mr. Bolton smiled pleasantly through Tennie's saltiness. "But don't they ever get tired of living small, Tennessee? Of just making do?" Mr. Bolton asked, his too-white dentures gleaming in the sun. "There's so much opportunity available for those who aren't too squeamish to reach out and take it."

"I don't see a thing wrong with living small, personally."

Mr. Bolton leaned close enough for Tennie to smell his stale coffee breath and chewing gum. He dropped his voice. "A word of advice? Aim higher. Don't get stuck here until you're old. And run over anyone who blocks you on your way out." Behind them, the back door opened. Mr. Bolton straightened and chuckled as if Tennie and he had just shared a good joke.

Tennie smiled weakly for Mimsy's sake, but her gloved hands tightened at her sides.

"Who wants to mosey down to town with me?" Mimsy called. She wore a flowing skirt and a nice pair of heels already, which meant they were *going*. "We can grab us a bite to eat and get a couple of spare keys made."

"A *couple* of spare keys?"

"One for you, and one for Mr. Bolton, since he practically lives here anyway."

Tennie made a face behind their backs.

"Maybe we'll just step into the jewelry store, too, and see what's shiny." Mr. Bolton winked, and Mimsy scoffed playfully, slapping his arm.

Tennie reluctantly ran inside for her wallet. When she came out onto the porch, Mimsy was waiting as Mr. Bolton started the car. Tennie winced at the still-shredded screen door.

Mimsy patted Tennie's arm. "I can read you too well, Storybook. I know you're not crazy about Mr. Bolton, and I'll admit he's rough around the edges. But he's sweet, and your ol' Mimsy could use someone to look out for her. An' opportunities don't knock often at my age."

"Mimsy, don't say that! You're wonderful!"

"Well, thanks, darlin'. I agree. It's just I'd hate to end up a burden to your mama and dad as I get on in years. And Mr. Bolton is a sensible choice, in a lot of ways, even if he's not your Poppy."

Tennie swallowed hard and nodded. "You could never be a burden, Mimsy."

"Neither could you, my Storybook. I always want the best for you."

Soon, the three of them rumbled their way down to town in Mimsy's car. Tennie was quiet. She didn't care for Mr. Bolton's attitude about Mimsy's home much. As a matter of fact, a few minutes ago she'd hoped French Fry would circle around the garden and decorate his jacket. *But Mimsy seems to like him and there's no accounting for taste*, Tennie reminded herself.

Besides, he might be the only thing that lets Mimsy keep her house and her property, Tennie thought bitterly. It was a deal with a snobby devil, but some things were worth it, she reckoned. She uncrossed her arms and gazed out the window as they turned onto Main Street.

The town bustled with life, and the corner of every block was decked out in gourds, hay bales, and bundles of leathery cornstalks. In a big field outside the main stretch—the same lot where Tennie had bought a precut Christmas tree with Poppy once—there was a gigantic corn maze with a big wooden lookout platform at its center. Stretched over the street between two light poles was a hand-painted bunting proclaiming "Happy Hollow-een!" *They're gettin' ready for the festival we're going to on my birthday*, Tennie thought wistfully. Her *thirteenth* birthday. It had all the makings of being a perfect one, if Tennie could get her act together.

She and Fox had two days to smooth out all the ghost wrinkles.

"What are you hungry for, Storybook?" Mimsy called over her shoulder.

Tennie's heart sped up. "How about pizza?" Fox couldn't dodge Tennie's ghost questions if they talked in person, she reasoned, setting her jaw.

"Pizza it is," Mimsy said, swinging the car into Pie in the Sky's parking lot. *I can help Fox finish their chores*, Tennie schemed. *We'll get 'em knocked out, and then we'll tackle the ghost problem.*

As soon as they stepped into the restaurant, Tennie's eyes combed the counter and booths for one of Fox's bright shirts, hands clammy inside her gloves. It was busy. The college-aged hostess at the counter didn't look thrilled to see them, scowling at Mimsy and Mr. Bolton.

"Why don't you go find us a table?" Mimsy suggested.

Tennie nodded. She did a quick sweep of the dining room, eyes peeled for Fox. *They're prob'ly in the kitchen*, Tennie reasoned. She stood by the swinging kitchen door until a waitress with a big cart hustled through. Tennie peeked inside. There, Mrs. Sanchez-Griffin laughed with one of the cooks as he brought cling-wrapped mounds of dough from a walk-in fridge. She caught sight of Tennie.

"Tennie!" Mrs. Sanchez-Griffin smiled broadly as she strode out and enveloped her in a big hug. A lump instantly squeezed Tennie's throat—she missed her own mom's hugs but hadn't realized it until just then.

"Hey, Mrs. Fox's Mom," she wheezed while having her ribs smooshed.

"What brings you down here, lady?" Fox's mother asked, letting go and giving Tennie's arm a friendly rub.

"Mimsy and her . . . beau," Tennie said, gesturing toward the hostess line.

Mrs. Sanchez-Griffin's smile stiffened a bit. Then, she pursed her lips and turned her gaze back to Tennie. "When are we gonna see you up at the house again? You're welcome anytime!"

"Actually, I came to ask Fox about hanging out. Can I see them?"

"Well, baby, they're over at someone's house this afternoon, but they'll be back home around seven. Why don't you drop by then?"

Tennie's stomach went strange and stabby. "So, Fox hasn't been here today?"

"I let them sweet-talk me into giving them Fall Break off. You're only thirteen once." Fox's mom sighed. "Well, I gotta get back to it, baby. Come on over to the house tonight, if you want, and we'll fire up the ice cream maker!"

Tennie nodded and watched Fox's mom disappear into the kitchen. Then, feeling queasy, Tennie plopped into the booth where she and Fox had eaten a few days before.

Helpin' with chores at the restaurant, my furry left foot, she thought bitterly. She squeezed her cell phone hard. Why had Fox lied? They could've just *said* they wanted to hang out with other friends. Now, Tennie felt blindsided, hurt, and unzipped in front of everybody, and tears threatened to roll.

Mimsy and Mr. Bolton approached, carrying a plastic table number. "This booth's a little far from the windows, don't you think?" Mr. Bolton commented, scowling indignantly. Tennie tried to smile but choked instead.

"S'cuse me, Mimsy. Restroom," Tennie managed.

She rushed down the hallway into the bathroom, relieved to find it empty. Inside a locked stall, she let her hot tears spill. *Fox must think I'm a massive baby who gets her feelings hurt easy*, Tennie thought. It was the only explanation for her friend's lie. *Like when I tell Shi and Harper roller coasters are boring, because they're not tall enough to ride them yet. And,* judging by the gallons of ridiculous tears rolling down Tennie's cheeks, maybe Fox was right.

That's what you get for being selfish, Tennessee. She'd given herself permission to crave special attention from Fox, gotten greedy for adventure in the forest. Tennie had let herself imagine she was part of something bigger and braver than she really was. Every time she'd ever gotten grabby that way, it had always circled back around to nab her on the backside.

Tennie's face scrunched, stifling a miserable sob. And now what? Had she scared Fox away? She'd certainly tempted terrifying ghosts into stalking her, and her family had fallen apart while she went gallivanting through the woods, acting foolish.

The bathroom door squeaked open, and Tennie clapped a hand over her mouth. Two sets of high heels clicked across the tile, and the smell of older lady perfume wafted through the air. Through the crack around the stall door, Tennie could see Lynnette Bless-Her-Heart and a silver-haired woman in front of the sinks, fixing their lipstick in the mirror.

"Ilene has been out with him three times this week already. You ever seen such a gold digger, Roselle?" Lynnette gossiped, sucking her teeth. "He's been up at her place every other day this month."

Tennie's jaw clenched at "gold digger." Anyone who had known Mimsy as long as Lynnette ought to know better.

"From what I hear, hers ain't the only place he's been sniffing around," Roselle-in-the-polka-dot-dress answered. "He was up at that place on Graystone Mountain first. My Stuart said that Russell came down from there lookin' wilder than a sprayed roach. I reckon he got told off."

"Serves him right. Most folks will tell him to get lost," Lynnette Bless-Her-Heart chuckled. "But you can't tell Ilene nothin' about him—you know how she is. The women in that family are stubborn as two mules tryin' to tango."

"Lord bless us," Roselle agreed. "Let's just pray she sends him packin'. He don't hold a candle to her poor Harold, rest his soul."

Tennie's cheeks burned as the women swished out of the bathroom again. She hated gossip with the fire of a thousand suns. It stirred up pointless trouble, and folks tended to warp one another's stories beyond recognition. Like *they* knew a flying flip about secrets, or what to do with them. Hearing stories repeated about her family—or even about snooty ol' Mr. Bolton—well, it made her mad enough to spit. Mad and worried.

If folks in the Hollow were this ugly to outsiders like Mr. Bolton, how much worse would Mama's reaction be when she met him? Besides being from the Hollow herself, Mama was also a dyed-in-the-wool daddy's girl, and still got choked up whenever folks talked about Poppy. She'd grow hopping mad, too, whenever Mimsy would complain about how quiet Poppy got sometimes.

It was time to get back to what Tennie did best—smoothing down ruffled feathers and making sure everyone stayed fair with one another. Mama and Dad needed Mimsy's help, and Mimsy . . . well, she needed Mr. Bolton's. Annoying as he was, he seemed to love Mimsy. And if Tennie couldn't help them all play nice, who else was going to?

Her own hurt feelings about Fox could wait. She didn't have time to start a disagreement over Fox's lie. Tennie would just have to try and soothe the ghosts alone, and end their nonsense once and for all.

When she got back to the table, Tennie's pizza went down like lumps of flour, but she stubbornly forced the bites with gulps of Coke. Then, for the rest of the afternoon, she went on a texting campaign, telling Birch what a sweet fellow Mr. Bolton was.

He gave me $20 to spend while they ran errands

I can't wait for y'all to meet him

Make sure Mama gets lots of sleep before Friday

When Tennie got home that evening, she carefully stowed the unspent twenty in her suitcase, planning to give it to Harper and Shi on her birthday during the Fall Festival. The twins were easy to motivate with money and cotton candy, and she needed every Lancaster to be on their best behavior so they'd make a good impression on Mr. Bolton for Mimsy.

That evening, Tennie asked Mimsy if she needed anything done around the house. Mimsy led her up to Poppy's old painting room, and asked her to pack away his things. "It's time," she said, yanking boxes from the closet and assembling them. "Don't look so sad, sugar—he hardly spent time in this room anyhow. He was always off in the woods, painting like the world was gonna end tomorrow. During the autumn, I'd hardly see him at all, and I'd be stuck in this big ol' house alone."

Tennie had heard Mimsy gripe about this before. Mama hated it when she did. Tennie had been taught to resent it, too, but this time, she just felt sorry for Mimsy. Her grandmother's elegant face looked sad and unsure, and her shoulders slumped.

"Sounds lonely," she murmured, fumbling a canvas into the first box.

"That was your Poppy," Mimsy sighed, waving a hand.

Tennie wanted to protest that it really *wasn't* but kept her mouth shut. Instead, she reminded herself that lots of folks had loved Poppy's paintings and had even paid a fair amount for them. Poppy had been looking out for Mimsy, was all.

Mimsy left Tennie to get to work, but hurt kept rippling through her every time she thought of Poppy. Finally, fed up with herself, Tennie tied a mental rock to the sadness and let it sink to the bottom of her heart.

She got to dusting. Then, she carefully wrapped Poppy's finished paintings in sheets of painter's plastic before placing them upright in a couple of large boxes. *You'll come home with me*, she promised them. She glanced at the unfinished paintings propped against some crooked old easels, lush flashes of the forest that faded in to blank white canvas. It was sad, Poppy passing on before he'd had a chance to finish things that were important to him.

Kinda like those ghosts, she thought suddenly, *hanging round here 'cause they can't finish what they started, neither.* While she worked, she racked her brain for ways to help the ghosts rest peacefully, ruminating on the clues. There wasn't much to go on. *They'll come around again*, she decided. *And when they do, I won't run. I'll just stay put, watching and listening.*

Finally, it was late, and all that was left were Poppy's paintbrushes and his unfinished paintings. Somehow, packing these away felt like a trickier task. *I'll do them soon*, she told herself. *But not tonight.*

She hoped Mr. Bolton would take the room's quick progress as proof that a Lancaster wasn't afraid to roll her sleeves up. *We're a good family. We're a hardworking family.* If Mr. Bolton saw that, he could even find a job for Dad at his company . . . doing whatever it was Mr. Bolton did to pay for bathrooms with waterfalls in them.

One last time before she went to sleep, Tennie sneaked a peek at her new texts. There were none.

"It's fine," she promised herself. Tomorrow morning, she'd go into the woods alone.

CHAPTER 13

Whittlefish woke Tennie in the middle of the night by sitting directly on her face and growling in rage.

"Get off, you rotten ol' thing," Tennie croaked, shoving him off. Whittlefish curled his injured leg to his chest, blinking slowly at her in indignation. Tennie's heart softened. "Sorry. I forgot about your paw." She checked the alarm clock.

"It's four in the morning! And you're not s'posed to be on the bed." Whittlefish pressed against Tennie's side and rumbled, the end of his tail flicking back and forth in agitation. When Tennie tried to shoo him toward the door, he hissed, retreating beneath the bed. He backed into a corner and refused to budge.

"Ugh, silly cat." Since she was awake already, Tennie sighed and decided to go visit the toilet. But as soon as she touched the freezing doorknob, the hair raised on the back of Tennie's neck.

Something . . . not alive . . . was on the other side of her bedroom door. Inside the house.

Not in the woods.

Not on the porch.

Inside.

Quietly as she could, Tennie locked the handle. *It won't do much good*, her reason told her. Eyes glued to the door, she walked backward toward the chair where she'd tossed her wool sweater. Fumbling it on over her sleep shirt, Tennie reminded herself of her plan: She was supposed to get closer to the ghosts, not farther away. She was supposed to set things right with them.

She had to open the door.

With a whimper, Tennie wished Fox was with her. *But Fox ain't here, and now I've got to be the brave one.*

Tennie walked toward the knob with outstretched fingers, shaking from head to toe and wincing at every creak of the floorboards.

"I'll do it on three," she whispered to Whittlefish. "One—"

she swallowed hard—"two, *three*." She twisted the handle slowly, then let the door swing open with a whining squeak. Then she waited.

Plunk, scraaaaaatch. Something thumped at her feet, then left a long, skinny scratch across the hardwood, disappearing into the darkness at the end of the hallway. *The watch ghost.* Tennie's courage almost abandoned her as heavy dread rushed in. Her ears began to ring, and black spots danced around the edges of her vision. One of her knees buckled, but she shot out a hand against the wall to steady herself.

I am watching and I am listening, Tennie repeated in her head like a prayer. Cold slithered in coils around her legs, and the watch ghost's deep, guttural howl vibrated through her chest. Its despair burrowed beneath her hair, her skin, her bones, and into her soul, sucking her toward its desolate nothingness like a whirlpool. Tennie felt hot and cold at once, and her thoughts jumbled.

A long hiss sounded from the puddle of shadow, then something invisible hit Tennie in the stomach, hooking itself hard into the edge of her cotton nightshirt where it peeked out from under her sweater. It yanked, and in horror, Tennie watched the fibers snag and snap, a hole ripping in the knit. That was enough watching and listening.

Dizzy and clammy, Tennie stumbled through the doorway of Poppy's painting room. She ran to an art easel, snatched up a handful of Poppy's paintbrushes, and clutched them to her pounding chest like an amulet, letting Poppy's gravel-pit voice hum through her head. The nothing-feeling hovered in the doorway, and Tennie scrambled in between boxes of Poppy's finished paintings. "You might be able to rip my shirt, but you can't have my mind again," Tennie spat.

The sticky nothing feeling crept into the room, then paused in front of Poppy's easels. It came no farther. Tennie's fingers clenched the paintbrushes. The watch ghost didn't move. Tennie sank to the floor and stared at the spot where the nothing had settled in the moonlight. Minutes stretched into an hour. Through the paintbrushes, Poppy's voice hummed and sang in her head, like a lullaby. Tennie fought not to rest her eyes, but gradually, her racing heart slowed, and she let her heavy head tilt back against the wall.

Tennie didn't intend to fall asleep. But as she stubbornly outwaited the swirling despair, her eyelids closed, and her breathing evened. *What will the waves wash up next?*

When she opened her eyes again, the room was full of sunlight and dust motes, and she could hear Mimsy stirring in her bedroom through the wall. There was no ghost. Looking down through sleep-blurred eyes, Tennie saw that her nightshirt was whole without a single rip. She stretched her aching legs and teetered to her feet.

She crossed the room. Gasping, she saw Poppy's unfinished paintings no longer had spots of blank canvas. Instead, in the half-done landscapes that Poppy would never complete were black charcoal markings, filling in the blanks. The art wasn't as perfect as Poppy's, but it was good enough to understand.

On the center canvas, Poppy's vernal forest crumbled abruptly into piles of stripped and shattered trees, their branches cracked at angry, jutting angles. On the left, the front half of a beautifully painted white-tailed buck ended in a pile of smeary bones.

"Dead forest," Tennie murmured. Did it mean Poppy's forest? *Her forest?*

The third, and smallest, was of a cottage in the woods. The sky billowed black and gray clouds of ash, and drawn into the window of the cottage, an old face stared out with a withered hand against the glass.

"Is that you?" Tennie whispered. "Are you the watch ghost?"

"Tennessee Marie Lancaster, I need a word with you!" Mimsy's voice rang up the stairs.

Tennie frowned at the sound of her middle name. "Coming, Mims!"

Tennie ran to her room and changed her clothes, then tried to coax Whittlefish into coming downstairs for his breakfast. He hissed, refusing to leave her bedroom.

Tennie hurried downstairs, screeching to a halt as soon as she entered the kitchen. Her first thought was that maybe the twins had arrived at Mimsy's house a day early, because the room looked like a tornado had hit a bakery. The counters and floors were strewn with cornmeal and flour, and messy ribbons of chocolate sauce dripped from walls. Tennie grimaced at over a dozen eggs smashed across difficult-to-clean places. In the middle of the floor, drawn in the dusting of flour, was an unfortunate caricature of Mr. Bolton wearing a twirly moustache and horns.

Underneath in tidy, cursive handwriting were the words *Eat Dirt*. Tennie gaped down at the drawing in horror. Mimsy put her hands on her hips. "Well?"

"You don't think . . . you can't believe *I* did this," Tennie stammered, her face growing hot.

The smell of heavenly cinnamon floated through the room. Without a word, Mimsy walked over to the oven, where a tray of her famous cinnamon rolls rested, and pointed. In the center of each roll rested a single, muddy marble.

"Honestly, Storybook, I don't know what to think. What's gotten into you? Run grab me the broom before Mr. Bolton comes in here and sees—" she waved her hand at the rude flour portrait.

"Before I see what?" Mr. Bolton's voice boomed from the doorway.

"Saints preserve us," Mimsy sighed, putting a hand to her forehead. Tennie smoothly scuffed her foot across the Mr. Bolton drawing, erasing its face.

"We were vandalized, Mr. Bolton," Tennie said, somewhat truthfully.

"Should we call the authorities?" he asked, frowning.

"I don't think that's necessary," Mimsy answered, giving Tennie a pointed look. "I imagine the culprit will feel guilty enough about it, by and by. And when they come 'round, I'll have them clean it up and give them a few odd jobs, for penance."

Tennie shrank inside, even though she knew the ransacked kitchen wasn't her fault. Not directly, anyway.

"Well, I'll tell you one thing," Mr. Bolton grunted, frowning. "This house isn't safe for you, Ilene. You shouldn't be living up here alone. The more I think on it, the more I'm convinced it might be time to sell this place."

No!! Tennie's heart screamed. "It's not dangerous here at all, Mr. Bolton! The truth is—"

"The truth is—" Mimsy cut in sharply "—if I sell this place, it won't be because I'm too old and frail to look after myself."

Mr. Bolton took Mimsy's hand. "Of course not, my dear! Forgive me for overstepping. How can I improve your morning?"

"Seein' as breakfast is spoiled here, I could use a nice cup of coffee from the diner," Mimsy sighed. "Would you mind terribly starting the car?"

Mr. Bolton kissed Mimsy's cheek. "That sounds just fine. I need to pick something important up in town, anyhow."

When he was gone, Mimsy put up a hand to stop Tennie from making up some explanation for the trashed kitchen. "You know well as I do that vandals didn't draw an ugly portrait of Mr. Bolton and strew flour from here to kingdom come. I don't know what this is about, Storybook, but you and I are gonna have a talk about it."

Tennie stared at the floor, ears aflame. "Yes, ma'am."

"I want this kitchen clean before I come back this afternoon. Now, let's see how far you got last night." Mimsy strode from the kitchen and up the stairs. Tennie scurried behind her, heart in her throat. *Don't be headed where I think you're headed*, she pleaded in her head. If Mimsy saw what the watch ghost had done in Poppy's old art room . . .

Mimsy marched into the studio, skirt swinging, then froze in front of the easels. Tennie cringed as Mimsy took in the macabre charcoal drawings the ghost had added to Poppy's unfinished paintings. After a moment, she cleared her throat.

"This . . . is very upsetting, Storybook."

"Mimsy, I—"

"Seems something's bothering you that you would do a thing like this. Why don't you open up to Mimsy? Tell me how I can help!"

Tennie stared at her shoes, unable to come up with an excuse. How in the world could she begin to explain? Her hands began to shake.

Mimsy sighed. "You're like your mama, sometimes. She never would let anybody help her with anything." Tennie's cheeks stung because that was a little true. Mama was proud, and it hurt that Mimsy thought the same of Tennie. "I'd like you to finish up in here before your folks come over tomorrow night. And no more acting out, do you hear? Things are workin' out with me and Mr. Bolton, and I'd like to keep it that way."

Tennie wanted to reassure Mimsy that she was on her

side, and that she was doing her hardest to make everything right. But the words stuck to her tongue. She nodded, sniffling. "Yes, ma'am."

Just as Mimsy turned to go, Tennie blurted, "You wouldn't really sell this place, would you?"

A sad look passed over Mimsy's face. "Don't you worry about that, darlin.' I'll cross that bridge when I have to. Now get to sweepin,' so I don't have to call your folks."

CHAPTER 14

Tennie scrubbed the kitchen until
her knuckles were angry and raw, and every last crack and
crevice was free of the sticky mess the marble ghosts had left.
Then she steeled her heart and hustled through packing the
rest of Poppy's canvases and brushes into boxes, taping the lids
shut with resolve. This was for her family, and Poppy would've
understood.

Exhausted and grubby, Tennie carried the tray of half-
spoiled cinnamon rolls onto the back porch. French Fry flapped
down from the trees and into the garden with something colorful in her beak. "Oh, heck no," Tennie shouted. "Stay away!
I'm not taking any more haunted gifts from crows."

Plopping onto the porch, she plucked a marble from a roll and lobbed it across the yard and into the forest. She hollered at the top of her lungs: "I don't know what you're playing at, ghosts! I was trying to *help you* to be at peace! I was listening!"

Tennie rage-ate one of the buns, tearing into it with bared teeth. "Anyway, I saw the disturbing drawings your sad little watch-friend left in Poppy's art room. And the drawing you left on Mimsy's floor. Y'all are just a bunch of creepy Bob Ross wannabes, aren't ya?"

She hurled another marble and bit into another roll, angry tears pricking her eyes. Yelling felt *good*. "And anyway, my lying, rotten friend Fox—who apparently thinks I'm too clingy—ain't here to help me figure out what the heck y'all are trying to tell me."

Tennie crammed the remainder of the second bun into her mouth and lobbed another marble at the trees. "So if you want my help, y'all have to start *being helpful to me*!!"

"*Ouch*," came a voice from the forest. Tennie startled, then relaxed as Fox emerged from behind a maple, a hand to their head. "Geez, your throwing arm is lethal, Tennie."

Tennie brushed the crumbs off her shirt and wiped her eyes, heart hammering. "How long have you been standing out there?" she demanded, pulling her wool gloves from her pocket and tugging them on.

"Long enough to find out I'm a lying good-for-nothing, I guess," Fox said, quirking their mouth sideways.

"You can't make me feel bad because *you* eavesdropped. It's not *my* fault you lied."

"Wow. You're a better guilt tripper than my mom."

"I'm just describing the situation," Tennie huffed, gathering up the cinnamon roll tray. "If you feel guilty about that, it's none of my business." She turned to go back into the house. *Fox is here*, she scolded herself. *You need their help. Why are you leaving?*

"Why're you here?"

"French Fry stole one of my maybe-haunteds. And . . . I was kinda hoping you'd be here. My mom said you came by the restaurant. I felt bad about not texting you back."

Tennie sniffed, staring at the cabin. She wanted to show Fox she was listening but couldn't make herself budge.

She could hear Fox tromping up the back-porch steps. "I don't blame you for being upset."

Tennie's hand froze on the knob. "I'm listening."

"I shouldn't have lied about not being able to hang out."

Tennie turned to see Fox staring at their shoes. "Then

171

why'd you do it? Do you think I'm too sensitive? 'Cause I don't need to be coddled or lied to."

"What? No! It's not like that at all. It's just . . ." Fox's face scrunched. They sat down on the top step. "Ughhh, this is hard. It's just you were so obsessed with helping the ghosts move on. And I hate that idea."

"You wouldn't hate it so much if they showed up on your front porch. Or in your hallway. Or if they wrecked your family's kitchen, and you got blamed for it!"

Fox's eyes bugged. "Whoaaa. They came inside your *house*?"

"Yes! And if I don't stop the ghosts from causing more trouble before my family gets here tomorrow . . ." Tennie trailed off, unsure what else to say. How could she explain her family's personal business to Fox without violating the rules of the Pride Wars? And so much depended on Tennie keeping things peaceful between everyone; it was like a thousand tangled threads. Hard to explain, even if she wanted to. "I just need to get this fixed."

Fox hugged their knees. They sat stiller than normal, chewing their lip. "Was your grandma hacked off about her kitchen?"

"Worse." Tennie frowned. "She was *disappointed*. Those

ghosts threw flour all over her kitchen like it was beads at Mardi Gras. It embarrassed her socks off. In front of Mr. Bolton." Tennie's bun-filled stomach roiled as she remembered the look on Mimsy's face.

"That sucks," Fox said, frowning back.

"That's why we need to figure out what the ghosts are saying! It's something bad—that's obvious. And it has to do with the forest."

Fox squirmed on the step, fidgeting. Their eyes darted nervously around the garden like they were looking for an escape route.

Tennie scowled. "You're gonna run off again, aren't you? You look like a cat in a shower."

Fox flinched. "Thinking about death and depressing stuff is . . . hard."

Tennie blinked, shaking her head. "You have ghosts doodled all up and down your arms! You're, like, the 'sorceress of spooky,' remember?"

"Yeah, when it's *fun*. Not when it feels so much like—" Fox bit their lip and held their breath, like the last word was too dangerous to set free. Tennie felt an annoying wave of empathy douse her anger.

"Endings?"

"Yeah, that."

"So, are you leaving, then?" *Please don't go*, Tennie wished.

"Not yet. I still have to get my maybe-haunted thing from French Fry," Fox said sheepishly. Tennie's heart sank.

"C'mon. I'll help you." Blinking back tears of disappointment, Tennie grabbed a cinnamon bun and strode into the garden. Why was she helping Fox leave faster? Why was she always so useful?

"Trade you!" she called to French Fry. The crow relinquished her trinket easily—it was a tiny ceramic unicorn with painted eyelashes too big for its face. When Tennie handed it to Fox, they lifted it to their lips and kissed it, crow germs and all.

I bet that unicorn was their sister's, too, just like the rest of their un-haunted objects, Tennie thought. Suddenly, Tennie had a desperate, last-ditch idea to keep Fox interested in staying. *I've got nothing to lose now*, Tennie thought. *They're going to leave anyway.*

"I have something wild to tell you, Fox. And I'll understand if you hate me after," Tennie said, tugging off a glove.

"Okayyy," Fox said, raising an eyebrow.

Tennie drew a deep breath. "I can do more than release

ghosts out from spooky stuff. I can . . . I can pull memories out of things. With my hands."

Fox giggled. "Sure, and I can turn cafeteria food into Spicy Cheetos and Oreos."

Tennie frowned fiercely, jutting out her chin.

Fox stared, eyes widening. "Wait, seriously?"

"I wouldn't joke about it, Fox. It's a pain in my backside. I'd stop if I could."

Fox ran their hand through their hair in excitement, and Tennie felt giddy. It was weird, having her secret out in the open. "Holy crow, Tennie! This whole time you've had a super-power! And you've been holding out on me?"

Tennie fiddled with her glove, guilt building in her chest. Fox was reacting exactly how she'd hoped—like a kid in a candy store. But Tennie felt awful for tempting them to stay by dangling her superburden like a shiny object.

"Here, try this one!" Fox held out the ceramic unicorn.

"Fox . . . not all memories are *good* memories," Tennie hedged, tensing.

"This one will be good. Promise."

Tennie swallowed hard. *Please be a nice memory*, she wished. *I don't want to upset my friend.* She'd lie about it, if she had to, to keep Fox from hurting. She grazed her fingers against the ceramic.

A little girl with long pigtails lay in a hospital bed, giggling. "Do it again!"

Memory-Fox bobbed the unicorn along the bed rail, talking in a goofy horse voice. "What do you call unicorn dandruff? 'CORN FLAKES!'" The little girl laughed and booed, and memory-Fox's chest filled with happy butterflies. This was Fox's happy memory.

Tennie pulled her hand away, feeling like a thief. "Unicorn jokes."

Fox's eyes shone extra bright. "My little sister loved that figurine. I was always planning to give it to her, eventually. She used to love it when I told goofy jokes with it."

"Used to?" Tennie asked, even though she'd already guessed the answer. Fox's sister had passed away. That's why Fox kept their box of maybe-haunted stuff.

The sad look clouded Fox's face. "She got sick . . . It'll be two years since her funeral this April. Can . . . can you show me the memory? Like when I helped you see the ghosts?"

"I have no idea," Tennie said slowly. "I've never tried before. No one else knows about my . . . well, I call it my superburden."

"You've never *told anyone*? Not even your family?"

"They wouldn't be thrilled to find out I can snoop through their memories," Tennie explained, shoulders tensing. "I can't even control it—that's why I have to wear gloves! They'd think I was a freak."

"Well, I don't think that." Fox bumped Tennie's shoulder with theirs. "Could we at least try?"

For a long minute, Tennie considered the terrible idea that she could use Fox's memory as a bargaining chip: She'd agree to let Fox see the memory *only if* Fox stayed around to help Tennie brave the ghosts. Almost immediately, she felt ashamed of herself. How horrible would Tennie feel if she lost the twins or Birch? It would be downright evil to dig into that tender spot in Fox, no matter how desperate Tennie felt.

"Give me your hand," Tennie said softly. Fox slid their hand into Tennie's, setting off sparklers in Tennie's chest.

"On the count of three," Tennie said, reaching for the unicorn. Fox counted them off, and then Tennie plunged into Fox's memory of Lola and the hospital bed, unsure whether Fox was seeing it, too.

When the memory ended, Fox was crying with a hand clapped over their mouth. Tennie threw her arms around them and squeezed hard. "I miss her so much," Fox mumbled into

Tennie's hair. "I kept hoping one of my maybe-haunted things would . . ."

"I know. I figured."

"But I don't think she's here anymore," Fox said, voice muffled.

Tennie thought for a long moment. "If I had to guess, I'd reckon that means she was happy," she whispered finally. "The ghosts that stick around, not so much. You wouldn't want her tortured that way."

Fox pulled away, wiping their face on their elbow. "Feelings are dumb."

"The worst," Tennie agreed. *And now, you're gonna leave me here alone with mine*, she thought, rubbing her tired eyes. "I get why you wouldn't want to stick around and talk with the ghosts. I mean. It makes sense."

Fox choked. "You've been trying to *talk* to them?"

Tennie flushed. "Yes. Sort of. So? You talk to your abuela's ghost!"

"That's different! She only ever yells about stuff burning in the oven. That's her loop, fire prevention. I'm pretty sure it's why she sticks around—grandmas are stubborn like that! But I don't think ghosts actually *converse*, Tennie."

"It worked when I talked to the watch ghost in Mimsy's hallway. It drew things on Poppy's unfinished art!"

"You followed the *watch ghost* into your *hallway*?" Fox muttered something in Spanish, shaking their head. "Okay, you need your ghostbuster badge revoked."

"It's not like I had a choice! If you got better ideas, I'm all ears."

"Anything's a better idea than you chasing that creepy-butt ghost by yourself," Fox spat, then heaved a big, resigned sigh. "Okay. You need supervision. We're gonna need a pen and paper and your Mimsy's internet password."

"You're staying?"

Fox knitted their eyebrows. "I guess I am."

CHAPTER 15

For the next hour, Tennie sat on her bed and recounted every tiny detail about the ghosts and what they'd done in the past two days. Fox nodded and scribbled furiously, pacing around with their tongue poked out.

When they were done, Tennie took the jumble of notes and ordered them into a neat list that read:

1. Marble ghosts played creepy chase on the porch. One of them screamed (like it did in the woods), the ground shook, and mud went everywhere.

2. I think they're sisters.

3. Their note said, "It's happening again, dead forest."

4. The watch ghost finished Poppy's forest paintings to show the woods looking creepy.

5. The marble ghosts wrecked Mimsy's kitchen and drew a rude portrait of Mr. Bolton, probably to get me in trouble.

6. Are they mad at me for not figuring it out fast enough?

7. Their notes disappeared, but Mimsy's kitchen mess was permanent. <u>GETTING STRONGER</u>.

"Okay," Fox said. "Now we need the internet password. We're gonna see if we can find news articles to match any of this stuff."

"It's 'praisethelard41316,'" Tennie instructed. Fox pecked the password into their phone.

Leaning over Fox's shoulder, Tennie directed as they googled every combination of words they could think of including *marbles*, *sisters*, *mud*, *dead forest*, and finally just *Howler's Hollow*. Besides some outlandish witch lore from the Hollow during its butter-churning days, there wasn't much in the way of online records.

"What we need is old-timey Google," Tennie announced, flopping back onto the bed.

"Which is . . . ?"

"A bunch of old gossips," Tennie said, raising a mischievous eyebrow.

"I know exactly where to find one of those." Fox grinned. "C'mon."

Tennie's heart skipped as the two of them borrowed old bicycles from Mimsy's shed and started down the mountain. Mimsy would be madder than a wet hen if she came back to find her gone while Tennie was supposed to be repenting for the kitchen mess. *But it's for the whole family's good, Mims,* Tennie thought, peddling hard. Crisp, sweet-scented air whooshed around Tennie's face, and behind her, Fox whooped in delight as they whizzed down the roads.

The whole way to town, Tennie prayed they wouldn't meet Mimsy's car on the way down the mountain, and, thank the stars, they didn't.

Fox skidded to a halt in front of the downtown tea shop, Some Like It Hot. Tennie carefully leaned her bike against the brick building and followed Fox inside. As soon as the doorbell jingled, Lynnette Bless-Her-Heart's drawn-on eyebrows shot up to meet her carrot-colored hair.

"Well, hey, baby!" she greeted Fox. A little bulldog jumped from its bed behind the counter and yipped ecstatically. "It's been a while since you came in!" Lynnette's eyes slid over to Tennie. "And Tennessee Lancaster, Lord, how you've grown! Your Mimsy's pictures don't do you justice!" Lynnette glided around the counter with arms outstretched, the skin under her arms waving hello. "Let me hug your neck!"

Tennie found herself smothered in pearls and leopard print bosoms for a moment, gasping for breath and being treated to a lungful of chemical gardenias.

"We have a question for you, actually, Miss Lynnette," Fox cut in casually. "I'm doin' a project on local history for social studies. But I lost my assigned article and don't want to get into trouble with my teacher."

Lynnette clucked her tongue. "Well, you've come to the right place. I reckon I know as much about Howler's Hollow as any history text." She winked, finally releasing Tennie.

"It was a story about sisters," Tennie said, smoothing her hair. "They may have died—we can't remember. And there was something about an earthquake, maybe, and some mud?"

Lynnette furrowed her brow. "Now, I don't remember anything like that happening in the Hollow. But seems I remember a newspaper article from—oh, thirty, thirty-five years ago—about an accident across the state line, in Virginia. Some children were playing marbles in a parking lot, and there was a mudslide, Lord rest them. I think they were both from the same family."

Tennie exchanged somber looks with Fox. "That's horrible."

"But it wasn't an earthquake. It was a dynamite blast, I think."

"Dynamite?"

"Mountaintop removal. Bigwigs used to ride in on a white horse, offerin' folks money for mineral rights to their land. Folks would take it, course, because it looked like an answer to a prayer. And then the bigwigs would chop the forests down around their ears and blast the top of the mountain off to get to the coal inside it."

"Dead forest," Fox said under their breath, nudging Tennie.

Lynnette folded her hands. "They did more than four hundred mountains that way. The constant blasting was enough to

184

put whole communities out of business forever. Anyway, that caused the mudslide, and buried those poor young'uns."

"I think I've heard enough," Tennie said. Her mind flashed to the mud oozing from the cracks in Mimsy's porch. She felt light-headed.

"Seems like a morbid topic for a school project," Miss Lynnette sighed, tossing a biscuit to her dog to stop its yapping. "Now, if you ask me . . ."

Fox steered Miss Lynnette's chatter around to goodbyes, and Tennie followed numbly, dazed. *Is that all the ghosts want to tell us?* Tennie wondered. *Their story?* That seemed easy enough. She'd let them know she understood, and that she was sorry it had happened.

Biking back up to Mimsy's took twice as much time and effort, so neither Tennie nor Fox talked much until they arrived in Mimsy's yard, sweaty and hungry. When they rolled into the driveway, Tennie groaned. Mimsy's car was back, Mr. Bolton's was still there, and . . .

"Oh no," she croaked when she caught sight of her family's dinged-up minivan.

"Whose car is that?" Fox asked, wiping sweat.

"That's our van," Tennie groaned. "My whole family is here a day early!" *Please don't let Mimsy tell them about the kitchen mess*, Tennie prayed. *And don't let Mimsy and Mama start in nitpicking each other. And don't let the twins misbehave! Or let the ghosts pull any more nonsense!* She hoped the Lord had a pencil and paper handy.

"Wait here for a second," she told Fox. Then with her lungs still burning and her sweaty hair stuck to her forehead, Tennie charged inside, hoping for the best.

She found Birch sitting on the rug in Mimsy's living room, his sandy hair engineered into a mohawk with a mess of hair clips while the twins carefully dabbed black polish onto his fingernails. Tennie gave him a bemused look. Birch caught sight of her and glared. "It was the *only way*," he griped darkly. "Mom and Mimsy are in the kitchen. Dad and Mr. Stuffed Suit are talkin' in the backyard."

"Don't call him that," Tennie hissed. "The you-know-whos will copy you, and then we'll *all* be in trouble."

"Well, watch out—Mimsy's upset about somethin', but she won't say what."

"Tennie!!" the twins hollered, rushing around the sofa and nearly knocking Tennie to the ground. She gathered their heads close to her face, breathing in their oatmeal-and-grass little sister smell.

"You have a suntan," announced Shiloh.

"You're all sweaty, too," Harper lisped.

"And *you* lost a tooth!" Tennie gasped, cupping Harper under the chin. "Did you get a dollar?" Harper shook her head. "Well, after you finish Birch's hairdo, I have a present for you both."

They squealed and ran away, and Tennie walked into the kitchen, heart thumping.

"The kids' hair is looking awful scraggly," Mimsy was saying to Mama, and Tennie could feel Mama bristle from across the room. "We can carry them down to the barber this afternoon."

"Oh, let's figure out where my oldest daughter is first," Mama countered, smiling too sweetly. "Since *someone* didn't remind her to keep her cell phone on. But you've been so tied up entertaining Mr. Bolton, I can't say I'm surprised." *Shots fired.*

Mimsy looked hurt by Mama's comment but pursed her lips to hide it.

"I'm here, Mama!" Tennie chirped from the doorway. Mama and Mimsy turned in unison. "It's not Mimsy's fault I disappeared—I ran off biking with Fox and forgot to say something."

"That's alright, Storybook," Mimsy said, giving her a sharp look that said it really wasn't, but she wouldn't rat Tennie out.

Tennie winced, then crossed the kitchen to give her mama a hug. "Anyway, Mims, the twins won't let anyone cut their bangs but me, so a trip to the barber won't do much good. I'll do it tonight."

Mama kissed Tennie's forehead, relaxing. "That's true. And how about you? You look like you've been havin' a good time!"

"Course she's been havin' a good time," Mimsy snapped.

"Yep. I've been hiking in the woods a lot," Tennie agreed nervously.

Mama sipped some herbal tea and yawned. "I used to love doing that, too, when I was your age. It was a nice break from all the chatter." Tennie noticed Mama's cuticles were picked ragged around her short fingernails. *It's gonna be okay, Mama*, Tennie thought.

Mimsy motioned for Tennie to follow her to the walk-in pantry. Tennie frowned, following. When Mimsy pulled Tennie inside and yanked the light string, her eyes were a mix of anger and deep worry.

"You did a real nice job on the kitchen, Storybook. And the spare room."

"Thank you, Mimsy."

"So what I don't understand is why you left such a nasty thing in Mr. Bolton's room."

"His room?" Tennie squeaked.

Mimsy yanked something from her apron pocket. It was the muddy Raggedy Ann doll, empty and limp. It was creepier than ever before, now with fresh tracks of mud-tears streaming from its cloth eyes. Tennie shuddered hard. Attached to its mildewing skirt with a rusty needle was a slip of paper with the scrawled words "Leave!"

"I haven't seen you act so childish since your eighth birthday, Storybook!"

"I swear, Mimsy, I didn't—" Tennie stopped talking and slumped in defeat, tears prickling. Nothing she could say about it would ever sound truthful. *I just have to fix it.* She balled her gloved fists in determination.

"I'll make it up to you. I promise! I want everything to go smooth for you and your beau, Mimsy. Just you watch." Tennie couldn't bear the look in Mimsy's eyes any longer, so she rushed into the kitchen with a serene mask pulled over her face. Mimsy followed, her dentures bared in a fake smile.

"Do you need help with the twins tonight, Mama?" Tennie crossed her fingers, hoping for a "no."

"Your daddy's about to take them for a hike," Mama said, yawning.

"I bet they'd love the playground downtown!" Tennie offered. She needed her family away from the house and the woods so she and Fox could banish the ghosts. *Now.*

"You're prob'ly right. I'll suggest it," Mama said, hands hugging her mug. "Mr. Bolton insists on taking us out for dinner, so we may as well head down that way."

"Can Fox stay the night?" Tennie asked. "We won't be trouble, I promise!"

Mama and Mimsy answered at the same time: "If it's fine with your mama" and "If it's fine with Mimsy!"

Tennie grinned. "Thanks." Then, rushing through the living room, she waved Fox inside from the porch and up the stairs.

Fox waved shyly at Birch on their way up. "Hey, Tennie's brother!"

"Hi, Tennie's friend."

"Your family's nice," Fox observed as they made it to the bedroom and locked the door.

"Nice enough," Tennie said. "Now we just wait for them to leave."

"Then what?" Fox asked.

"We wait for the marble ghosts to show up. They're nearby."

"How do you know *that*?"

"They pranked the guest room," Tennie muttered.

"Yikes."

"We just have to let them know we understand what happened to them," Tennie said, feeling dizzy. She raised the window for some fresh air, and her ears perked when she heard Dad and Mr. Bolton's voices in the garden below.

Mr. Bolton's voice boomed. *"Well, if you're ever looking for a job, son, I'm always looking for a good renaissance man at my company."*

Tennie watched her dad grow a wide, goofy smile. Anyone who didn't know Dad well would think he was pleased as peas with Mr. Bolton's offer. But Tennie recognized her dad's expression. It was his "Please, Lord, please help me not throttle this obnoxious fellow" grin.

Tennie breathed faster. *Yes!* This was exactly the sort of break her family needed. Dad could pay for a bigger place, Mimsy would be square financially, the forest wouldn't get sold, and Tennie could make sure Mama stayed in a good place. *"Be nice, Dad,"* Tennie urged quietly. *"And just say yes!"*

Fox leaned closer to the blinds, squinting. "Ugh, *that guy*," they whispered, making a face. "He came into Pie in the Sky last week and blessed the hostess out over a wrong dessert!"

"Shhh! He's just used to a different life, I think," Tennie hissed. "He's got some important job and is used to being in charge."

"That's no excuse to act like a wet sock," Fox said, making a gesture toward the window. "What's he *do* to make all that money?"

"I don't know, exactly," Tennie admitted. "But I'm hoping he can give my dad a job, since—" Tennie broke off and bit her lip. *Since Daddy's out of work again.*

"What's his name, even?" Fox said, sticking their nose in the air. "Tricorn Warren Goldenbricks the third?"

"His very *normal* name is Russell Bolton," Tennie huffed.

"Ha! Gotcha!" Fox crowed, whipping out their phone. "Now, we google him!"

"Fox, don't!" Tennie said, stomach turning.

"Why not? Don't you want to know who your grandma's dating?"

"Yeah, but . . ."

"Whoaaaa," Fox muttered. "This guy owns everything. There's got to be, like, fifteen giant businesses listed here."

"He's good at what he does, I guess," Tennie relented, sneaking a peek over Fox's shoulder.

Fox thrust the phone inches from Tennie's nose. "Geez, Tennie, *look*. His father owned a coal company."

"So?"

"And the marble ghosts drew him! He's even on our clue list!" Fox said, face going solemn. "I'm telling you, there's something off here."

"I'm *done* looking for trouble," Tennie muttered, hugging her arms across her chest. "We're supposed to be calming things down, not riling them up worse."

"He's been staying here, right? Then there's an easy way to settle this," Fox said, dropping their voice. "Go through his room and use your superpowers."

"What? No!"

"It's simple. Check his stuff for weird memories. If he's innocent, you don't have to worry anymore."

"Or I could talk to the ghosts first, and if that works, I won't have to!" Tennie insisted stubbornly. If she could put the ghosts to rest, that would keep her from finding out anything unsavory about her Mimsy's beau—especially anything that would make Tennie hate her family needing him so much. Sometimes, it was better not to know.

"Suit yourself."

CHAPTER 16

Almost by accident, Tennie managed to talk her parents into letting them stay home from the family outing. At first, Mimsy raised an eyebrow and asked whether Tennie "could handle the responsibility," no doubt recalling the mess in the kitchen. That triggered Mama's love of arguing, and it was an easy win from there. Mimsy gave Tennie a firm "Act sweet!" but didn't snitch, to Tennie's relief. Fox got permission to sleep over. So as soon as Tennie's family filed outside and the front door shut, the two of them walked from room to room, calling out to the ghosts.

When they had no luck inside, they put on their jackets and

shoes and wandered into the forest, searching for cold spots. But the forest seemed determined to hold its secrets, and the ghosts wouldn't show. They kept walking anyway, and somehow Tennie's hand found its way into Fox's, and the two of them walked in time.

She liked Fox. *Like*-liked. And she loved the forest, with every fiber of her being.

The leafy canopy convinced Tennie that everything would always be okay, and had always been okay, since the dawn of time. Each snaking root, spinning leaf, bobbing goldenrod, teeming bird's nest, and soaring branch were every bit as tangled as her family's troubles, but somehow, the forest's jumble made sense. There was a wild harmony to it, like her star-shaped hand in Fox's knobby fingers. So, what was the glue holding the wilderness together? If there was any, Tennie couldn't see it. It just *held*.

Why can't my family be that way? Tennie wondered wearily. She knew peacemakers were supposed to be blessed, but sometimes Tennie felt downright cursed. Someday, she'd run off into the forest, make herself a cabin, brew her tea, and live in peace. But it couldn't be today. Not when everything was falling apart because her family was determined to do things the hard way.

And the ghosts had picked now, of all times, to hide themselves.

"It's getting late," Fox said nervously. "My parents don't like me in the woods after dark. C'mon. We'll look again in the morning."

Disappointed and frustrated, they trudged home.

It wasn't long before Tennie's family plus Mr. Bolton got back from dinner. According to family tradition, Mimsy made brownies and everyone crammed into the living room to watch an old creepy movie, in honor of Halloween Eve. But every scary sound effect and dramatic scream made Tennie sweaty with worry that one of the ghosts had chosen the very worst moment to show itself.

Finally, everyone was divvied into separate rooms for the night—Dad and Mama in a room, Mimsy in hers, Birch and the twins on makeshift pallets in Poppy's newly cleared art room, Mr. Bolton downstairs, and Tennie and Fox sharing Tennie's room.

Fox conked out on the end of the bed waiting on a turn to brush their teeth, so Tennie covered them with a skeleton throw and softly whispered good night.

Then, Tennie lay awake, staring at the ceiling and waiting for something—a wave of cold, a scream from her siblings' room, a finger tracing down her back—but minutes stretched into hours, and nothing happened.

Finally, her eyelids turned to lead, and her feet found a warm spot on Fox's back. And soon she fell asleep.

In the cold, small hours, Tennie woke up curled in a ball. Fox was still sprawled out at the foot of the mattress, and to her left, one of the twins had sneaked into bed with them. For a while, Tennie was careful not to move a muscle—she didn't want to wake anyone. Finally, she inched her fingertips over to the side table and snagged her phone.

She found her brother's number.

You awake?

Almost immediately, Birch texted back.

Yep. Can't sleep.

Tennie grimaced at the pointy elbow in her back. A classic Shiloh-the-bed-hog move.

Will u come get Shi?
She escaped your room and I don't want 2 wake Fox

Birch responded with a single question mark and a photo: an angelic Harper and Shiloh, snuggled together like baby birds on their sleeping bag.

The elbow pulled away from Tennie's back, and her skin crawled as she slowly turned her head toward the girl-sized lump under the covers beside her.

The blanket rose and fell steadily. The form rolled over, ever so slowly, to face Tennie, its head buried in the covers. A scream stuck in Tennie's throat as a small, dirt-streaked hand inched out from under the blanket and pointed at the frosty window.

Tennie kicked her way backward, falling off the bed and onto the floor with a *whump*! She rose on bare feet and gathered every ounce of her courage. "I know what happened to you, marble ghosts. I'm real sorry about it. But now, I need you to *be at peace*," she said in a shaky voice.

The form on the bed rose, still covered in a blanket. Pale, filthy feet peeked out from beneath, treading slowly around the bed and to the window. Tennie's cold shoulders shook. A bluish hand reached out from the blanket, undoing the window latch, then lifting the sash.

"Dead forest." A flutter of wings filled the open window. French Fry landed on the sill, then cocked her head. The dirty

fingers contorted and twitched like something badly broken, cracking as they pointed out to the trees.

"What does that *mean*?" Tennie whispered, mouth dry.

The voice came strained and hoarse. *"Come and see."*

Something yawned in Tennie's belly. The crow flapped her wings and whooshed out into the yard, cackling. The dead girl under the blanket began to shrink, mud oozing out beneath the fabric and spreading across the floor.

A giggle came from the darkness behind her, then beside her, followed by a hollowing whisper: *"Come, silly girl. The trees have something to show you."*

A lump gathered in Tennie's throat. "Okay. If you'll leave my family alone, then I promise to listen," Tennie whispered. The room grew warm again.

Tennie ran to the window, looking out into the yard to see the crow waiting in the moonlight. Scrawled in mud across the windowsill were the words: *He's waiting.*

Tennie swallowed hard. She didn't need to ask who, because she could already feel the sad, hollow pull of him deep inside her gut.

CHAPTER 17

Tennie tied on her boots. She tiptoed across the room and put on her jacket, then armed herself with courage—and Poppy's walking stick. She held her breath and inched past Birch's door so he wouldn't catch her leaving.

Tennie had to do this alone. Fox wouldn't approve of Tennie going after the watch ghost, so Tennie left quietly. She wasn't about to pass up the chance to fix this mess, once and for all, before the ghost made trouble for her family.

Things were so close to working out. The Lancasters could have an okay life, and they could have it without a fuss. Tennie just needed to be brave and square with the watch ghost.

She crept down the stairs, through the kitchen, and onto the back porch.

"Caw, caw!" French Fry stared at Tennie with glittering eyes from the porch rail. Gleaming in the moonlight, the antique watch dangled from her beak. *Follow me.*

"Right," Tennie shivered, pulling her jacket tight. The crow took flight, and Tennie's legs churned along with her stomach as she ran toward the tree line.

"Tennie, what the heck are you doing?" Fox's groggy voice called from the porch doorway.

"The watch ghost," Tennie shouted, panting. "I have to find it, Fox!"

"Wait—my shoes!! Ugh, *dang it*!" Fox's voice faded behind Tennie, as she struggled to keep up with the flying shadow of the crow. She put her head down and ran harder. *Bye, Fox.*

Tennie knew the trail through the old woods well enough now—she hurdled a root here, anticipated a wobbly stone there—and hardly needed light to find her way. But the silver bowl of the moon spilled dappled, glowing pools on the trail just the same, and Tennie's heart hammered wild in her chest as she charged through them. Night air stung her cheeks, and brambles bit her ankles, but Tennie knew she couldn't slow. She was getting close.

A sad feeling in her gut began to tug, stronger and stronger, drawing her in. "*Caw-caw,*" French Fry called, goading her on, as if she could stop herself if she wanted to. *There's some big truth ahead*, she thought, *and I'm caught in its gravity.* She was losing herself in it.

French Fry perched in a tree above her, and a calm sort of dread settled over Tennie as she slowed to a stop and tried to catch her breath. The night breeze picked up and began to carry a soft, keening howl around its edges. This was it. "I'm here," she called.

Before the frost bit the leaves on the forest floor, and even before she felt the full rib-shaking rumble of the watch ghost's moan, Tennie felt its heaviness. She let her heart get caught up in it, swept like a twig in its deep, cold current. Several yards ahead in the shadows, a nothingness called to her, slow and mournful.

I'm listening, she thought. *I have to know.*

Something hit the ground in front of her feet. Tennie jumped back and gazed down, expecting to see a long scratch mark. She blinked in surprise. French Fry had dropped the watch. Tennie bent to pick it up.

"Tennie!" Fox's ragged voice panted from the path behind her.

I've got to know, haven't I? Tennie thought. She yanked off her gloves with her teeth. Then, she picked up the watch and, clutching it tight, walked straight into the arms of the hungry nothingness that waited in the shadows.

Tennie plunged into an icy river of memory.

The woods shone bright in the daylight around Tennie— not her forest, but a mountainside just the same, full of nodding wildflowers and birdsong. The steep slope she stood on was strewn with tender maidenhair ferns and electric blue irises. Down its middle cascaded a little waterfall attended by crimson-and-white jack-in-the-pulpit flowers. The clear water plunged into a pool at the bottom that teemed with minnows and bobbing watercress.

On the other side of the pool sat a young man with shaggy hair and a serious forehead, sketching away in a notebook. Something about him seemed familiar. But before Tennie could call her hello, the ground shook, knocking her off her feet.

The young man hesitated, frowning. For several long moments, he stood as if awaiting direction from the wind on how to proceed. When none came, he gathered his things and ran, even as Tennie called out to him. She followed him, running alongside the opposite bank of the creek. The water deepened, and as they hurried alongside it, the woods began to change. The trees became broken, then black and twisted.

The sky darkened. Instead of ferns and thimbleweed, bleaching bones littered the slopes around Tennie. Little empty cabins and cottages sat coated in black dust. The dead forest. She gazed across the empty water to see the young man was crying.

Tennie blinked to find herself on a sloping hill, overlooking a parking lot nestled in a neighboring ravine. The young man stood beside her, and Tennie was surprised to recognize him, finally: It was a young Poppy! He tried to whistle hello to the kids playing below, then coughed from the dust in the air. Then, the ground shook again. Poppy looked up in alarm just in time to see a wave of mud cascading down the side of the ravine, carrying rocks and trees with it. The little girls in the parking lot noticed too late, and Poppy raced toward them, praying as he went.

Then, Tennie sat in a courtroom. Poppy sat at a table wearing a shabby suit beside her, stammering angrily into an old-timey microphone. Poppy pointed at another young man— a familiar-looking devil with an oiled beard—and accused him of murder. "He's poisoned the whole town with his blasting! He's good as killed those little girls! He's a thief, a liar, and a cheat!" The judge slammed his gavel, shaking his head in regret. Poppy left the courtroom and sat on a bench outside, shoulders slumped.

Tennie tapped his shoulder. "Poppy?"

When the young man looked up, his face was wrinkled, like the old Poppy Tennie loved. But he carried a deep sadness in him that Tennie never remembered seeing there.

"My little Tennessee. I never wanted you to see me like this. I wanted to protect all y'all from the horrible things that happened to me when I was young."

"You never told anyone!" Tennie exclaimed. "No one knew!"

"Oh, Tennie. These woods, these mountains . . . they're precious, and I waited too long to fight for them. Once I finally worked up the courage to stand for the ones I was born to, no one else was left to stand with me. By then, I couldn't stop that rascal Bolton from blasting. So, I moved to the Hollow. And I worked myself to the bone to keep everything your Mimsy and I built together—our family and our home. I reckoned land was a thing I could write my name on, just like the other foolish fellas who came before me, right on back to the first European knuckleheads who stole it. I thought I could protect it if it belonged to me. And if I did, that sadness could never touch what I loved, ever again."

The words landed like hot coals in Tennie's heart. She couldn't look the watch ghost—Poppy's ghost—in the eye. Because Fox was right. This had been about Mr. Bolton all along, and Tennie had spread out the welcome mat for him, bound and determined he was her family's ticket to peace. She'd helped let him in.

Tennie thought of Mimsy, lonely during Poppy's long hours of work. How Mimsy was too proud to admit to her money troubles. She thought of Mama's blues, and how she never could seem to let folks in. She thought of Birch, who got blue sometimes, too, and was struggling to accept help with it. And . . . herself. She never could seem to stop worrying. "All of us, too hardheaded to lean on each other," she murmured.

When she looked up, Poppy's memory was fading fast.

"I think the sadness found us anyway, Poppy. That man, Mr. Bolton? He's here in the Hollow now, sniffing around our mountain. How do I stop him?" she asked.

"Wake up, Tennessee. Act ugly. Make trouble."

CHAPTER 18

A faraway rumbling tickled Tennie's
ears. Then a voice coaxed her back to her body. She was
freezing.

"Tennie!" Fox's voice cracked. Something shook Tennie's
shoulders. Her eyelids slid open and shut. Everything was dark,
with strange flashes of light. Cold rain hit her skin. "I hate this,
I hate it, I hate it," Fox muttered beside her. Their hands yanked
something from Tennie's damp jeans pocket.

Leaves hissed as wind whipped the trees. Tennie's mind
skipped like a rock on water. *Had Poppy been here? Was the
forest dead?* Each drop of rain from the sky hit her skin like
freezing fire. No, Poppy's ghost was gone. Tennie could feel

it, but his deep sadness had transferred to Tennie's own soul, dragging her down, down, down . . .

"Hello? Tennie's brother? This is Fox—we're on the trail in the forest, and your sister won't wake up. I tried but . . . I can't carry her. She's—hello? She's burning up," Fox sputtered, yelling over the spitting wind. Fox's voice was so sad. Tennie tried to reach out and squeeze their hand, but her arms wouldn't move.

Branches snapped. Fox whispered in Tennie's ear. Tennie couldn't make out their words for the rumbling around them— was it blasting or thunder? Then, she realized Fox was praying.

The sadness in Tennie's soul unspooled and surrounded her like a cloud. And deep inside its heaviness, she felt a flicker of *something* gather. Something like fire, burning her from the inside out.

"Aw, man, Tenn." Birch's voice was above her. His clumsy hand pushed hair off her face. She felt herself scooped into his arms, feet swinging. "What the heck *happened* to her?" Tennie felt her brother's heart pumping hard against her cheek.

Fox answered in a string of prattle Tennie's mind could not latch onto.

She wandered in and out of overlapping memories: a ninth birthday Mama had slept through. The hike when she almost told Dad about liking boys *and* girls, but volunteered to clean the garage instead. The day she quit the softball team, then the one when she'd stopped going to classes because of her super-burden. Trying to eat corn on the cob with gloves on. Long days at home, without going out. The forest and its wide, wild hills. Fox's laugh. Poppy.

Birch jostled her and hollered. Then, there were voices all around her—Mama, Mimsy, Dad. Someone grabbed her like a rag doll and hauled her up the stairs. Tennie's body sank into a soft bed. Mama hovered above her face, pulling back her eyelids and shining a bright light at them, looking at her fingernails, sticking a thumb to her pulse.

"My bag! In the van," Mama barked, then turned back to Tennie. "Hey—look at me, kiddo! There you are. Good girl," she kept saying.

Tennie blinked and started to come around. Then, through a long string of interrogating questions, Mama discovered Tennie hadn't had anything to drink that day, nor eaten much, despite biking all over "God's green earth" and "running off into the woods in the middle of a storm like a feral cat."

There were glasses of water and toast and fussing until, finally, Tennie was pronounced okay to sleep. "As long as you're *sure* she didn't hit her head, Fox," Mama asked pointedly. Fox reassured her that they'd hugged Tennie right as she fell.

Tennie was quiet through all of this, slowly organizing the ghost's stories into a proper timeline in her mind. Mr. Bolton—or his father, maybe—had ordered his mining company to blow up a whole mountain in Virginia decades ago. He'd tricked folks out of their land, like Miss Lynnette had said. His burning and blasting had poisoned a river and caused mudslides. Things got so miserable, folks left. Others, like the marble ghosts, got hurt. Poppy had tried to fight it in court, but by then he was too late to stop anything.

That's why Mr. Bolton was richer than Midas. And now, he slept in Mimsy's guest room downstairs. But what could she do?

Mama shooed everyone out of Tennie's bedroom.

"Can I stay?" Fox begged.

"*Only* if you let her rest."

As soon as Mama left, Fox sat on the floor next to the bed, resting their head against the mattress.

Tennie tried her voice. "Fox?"

Fox twisted around. Their eyes were red. "Yeah?"

"Why're you sittin' on the floor?"

"So I can stop you from runnin' off again," Fox muttered.

"I won't. I found answers. I know who the watch ghost was."

Fox climbed onto the bed, wide-eyed, and Tennie began to explain about Poppy's ghost. Then Tennie began to tell *her* story.

Warm tears streamed down her cheeks as she explained her family's troubles. Hot, angry words spilled out. How tired she was. How she wished her family could be honest with one another. And, most of all, how Tennie wanted this one thing—for her beloved forest, where she could run wild and be a little bit selfish, to be cared for and safe.

"Just tell your family that," Fox said when Tennie stopped to breathe.

"But I can't just *say* it. I'd have to tell them how I know all these secrets. Plus, Mimsy needs security and Daddy needs a job, and Mr. Bolton can help with both. Besides, it'd start World War III between Mama and Mimsy—me mentioning things they aren't proud of. And Mama would feel so bad to find out that—" Tennie's face crumpled.

"That her unbelievably helpful daughter isn't okay? 'Cause I'm pretty sure moms are supposed to care about that," Fox said, scowling.

"She does! I mean, she would!" Tennie argued.

"Okay. So?"

"That's why I can't ask for too much! They're already

doing their best," Tennie insisted, twisting her hands up in the blankets. "And I can handle it."

The first eerie morning light glowed through the window. Fox curled up in a ball beside Tennie and gazed up at the ceiling, sadness furrowing their forehead. "I'm gonna tell you a secret. A confession.

"My little sister, Lola, made friends with French Fry first, not me. She was patient like that. French Fry trusts me because of Lola, I'm pretty sure. Anyway, when Lola was in the hospital, I'd go see her every day to tell her how her crows were doing." Fox began twisting the faded friendship bracelet around their wrist.

This was it. Fox's sadness. Tennie held very still, afraid if she moved, Fox might stop talking.

Fox continued softly. "The day she—when it was her time to *go*?"

Tennie nodded.

"I was supposed to be getting snacks from the vending machine and come straight back to her hospital room. But I *left*, Tennie. I walked to the park. It was just too hard—" Fox swallowed. "I felt so afraid to be there. My parents didn't come find me, because my sister needed them." Fox's voice cracked. They hugged their knees closer.

"And I didn't let my grief sink in, just that guilt. Not until you told me Lola's maybe-haunted stuff wasn't . . . wasn't going to give me a second chance to say goodbye."

"I'm sorry," Tennie whispered. "I didn't mean to make it worse."

Fox sat up. "That's not the point! Feeling sad brought all these memories of my sister back. It's like a light came on. Here." Fox tapped their sternum. "It hurt, but it was a gift, too. Maybe that's what your family needs."

"To feel *sad*?" Tennie tensed.

"Well, yeah. It's better than you doing it for them."

"Watching them be sad is ten times worse! Like watchin' roadkill in slow motion. It'll be a disaster."

Fox waved upturned hands, exasperated. "Didn't you just say that after you came to Mimsy's, your parents noticed your brother was depressed? That seems *good*."

But what if I speak my mind—if I tell them what I think, not to mention what I can do—and it's too much for any of them to handle? Tennie worried, chest aching.

Fox sighed hard. "Anyway, if you don't say something, that jerk Mr. Bolton will weasel his way onto your property and ruin everything. Our forest. Your Mimsy's house. *My* house. Pie in the Sky. Howler's Hollow. You heard Miss Lynnette!

213

Mountaintop blasting poisons everything around it. But your gift has *proved* he's no good, Tennie. You can tell them the truth. And they'll have to believe you."

"What if they believe me, but they decide a deal with the devil's worth it?"

"Tell them it's important to *you*," Fox mumbled, yawning and closing their eyes. "It works with my folks. Family should care like that."

Make trouble, Tennessee, Poppy's ghost had said. The most troubling thing Tennie could imagine was *wanting* something. But what if Tennie spoke up for herself, and no one cared?

CHAPTER 19

A finger poked Tennie's shoulder.

"Hey, Bedhead. Breakfast is ready."

Tennie looked up to see Birch in flannel pants, holding a steaming mug. "Happy birthday coffee," he grunted, settling it on the table. The mug was topped with whipped cream and leaf-shaped sprinkles—a Lancaster tradition: coffee when you turned thirteen. Birch nudged her shoulder, then mumbled a soft "Glad you're okay" before leaving.

Tennie dressed. She brushed her hair. Everything was the same as always—except the yawning, hungry *want* in her gut that had nothing to do with breakfast. She felt sharp and awake and alive, even though her sorrow was still tender and ready to spill.

She walked to the hall closet and pulled out one of Poppy's flannel shirts, putting it on and rolling up the sleeves. Then, with her jaw set, she pulled her hair back into a tight ponytail and walked down the stairs.

Fox was in the living room already, rolling on the floor and play-roaring at the twins. The little girls shrieked and giggled in delight. Mr. Bolton scowled at them from the kitchen doorway. His sharp eyes were bloodshot, and his unshaven face was covered in strange scratches. Tennie narrowed her eyes.

"Good morning, Mr. Bolton."

"*Well*, Tennessee. I'd like a word with you and your parents, now that you've decided to join the land of the living," Mr. Bolton said loudly.

"Why's that?" Tennie asked, lifting her chin.

Whittlefish tried to scoot past Mr. Bolton, brushing against his leg, and Mr. Bolton used his shiny shoe to *kick Mimsy's cat*. Whittlefish growled and limped behind the couch.

It was that small act of meanness that struck a match and set off an explosion in Tennie's heart.

"How *dare you*?" Tennie seethed, crossing the runner rug. She grabbed a fake apple from Mimsy's decorative bowl and hurled it at Mr. Bolton. "How dare you come into my Mimsy's house and act so awful and ugly?!"

Shiloh and Harper froze, jaws dropping, and stared at their big sister. Fox grinned, and Birch, sitting on the hearth, raised an eyebrow over his coffee mug.

"My dear, I hardly think you're in a position to talk about bad behavior," Mr. Bolton said, walking toward Tennie. Those hateful, cocksure eyes of his fixed her with a cold warning. "Your grandmother may be too indulgent to correct you, but I think we both know you've caused plenty of trouble for one week."

Dad and Mama appeared in the kitchen doorway, frowning. Mimsy followed, too, scooping up Whittlefish and looking pale. Tennie's pulse hammered and her ears felt hot, but she wasn't about to back down. Not anymore. Poppy's shirt hummed softly in her mind. *What will the waves wash up next?*

The waves haven't washed up anything for me *to be scared of,* Tennie realized. They'd washed up the soul of Tennessee Lancaster, who had decided she wasn't content to wander her own life like invisible mist anymore. Her legs might feel weak and wobbly, but Tennie *wanted*. Tennie didn't shiver. She *burned*.

"You mean the mess in the kitchen? Or the screen door?"

"I'm talking about the very rude word you wrote in mud all over my briefcase this morning in the guest room. And my window, which you opened in the middle of the night. Yes, I saw your muddy handprints on the sill. Those infernal crows flew in, and the wretched creatures attacked me! I could have been blinded! You're reckless and inconsiderate, young lady."

"I don't think *you're* in a position to talk about *reckless*, Mr. Bolton. Not after the mess your company made of that mountain in Virginia thirty years ago. Not after your mudslide killed those girls."

Mama and Dad exchanged looks. Mimsy let out a soft groan, hand over her mouth.

It was like Tennie's words had ripped a mask off Mr. Bolton's face. His cheeks turned purple. Spit sprayed from his mouth as he spoke. "I have no idea what you're talking about. Why, if you were my daughter, I'd—"

"But see, I know what you're up to. You're trying to get Mimsy's woods. You want to tear them down and dig out the mountain to buy more fancy cars and big houses," Tennie yelled, her whole chest buzzing. "An' you don't give one hoot about my family, you hateful, old, used Band-Aid!"

"You'll soon find I can take better care of your family than anyone else has ever managed to," Mr. Bolton spat.

"Squeamishness over land is a poison. In my hands, this mountain can become something great!"

"In your *pockets*, you mean!" Tennie roared. "Anyway, what makes you think you can carve up the hills you came from, like they're nothing but Christmas turkey, and get away with it? That's practically eatin' your own mama!"

"Young lady," Mr. Bolton growled, stepping forward and winding up his open hand.

A fist clapped onto Mr. Bolton's wrist from behind. Dad gave him a gigantic, dopey smile. "Say one more word to my kid, and I'll pick you up and carry you out to your car personally, Mr. Bolton. Then, I'll roll you right off this mountain. Think of it as valet service. Free of charge."

"Get your filthy hands off me!" Mr. Bolton growled.

Mimsy crossed her arms and scowled at Mr. Bolton. "Get out. I've had enough of you."

"Ilene, this has all been a nasty misunderstanding. Surely you won't let the lying tantrum of a misbehaving child . . ."

"It don't matter if she's lying or not," Mimsy said, voice firm. She took something from the pocket of her slacks. "I've seen everything I need to make my decision, Russell. I'll thank you to take your ring back. I'd sooner marry a catfish."

Mr. Bolton glared. "Keep it," he snapped. "That shabby

diamond is the most money you'll ever see, foolish woman. There are other ways to lose a mountain. In the end, you'll wish you'd accepted my generosity." He stormed out of the house, slamming the door hard enough to rattle the trinkets on Mimsy's shelves, then sprayed gravel across the driveway as he sped away.

"He left his stuff here," drawled Dad.

"Dibs on his shirts," Birch quipped.

Mama put a hand on Mimsy's shoulder. "I'm sorry, Mother."

Mimsy scowled, eyes watering. "Well, I'm not, even though I ought to be. *Good riddance.* I could use a glass of brandy."

Mama hugged Mimsy, then stared at Tennie. "You wanna tell us what that was all about?"

Across the room, Fox mouthed, *Tell them!* Tennie's pulse raced. Her hands were hot and sticky inside her gloves.

"If everybody could sit, I need to show y'all somethin'." Tennie took several calming breaths as her family settled on hearth and rugs and chairs, staring. *What am I doing?* she thought as Fox excused themself to the back porch.

It felt weird, being the center of attention.

They expect me to smooth things over now. It's what Tennie did best. It's why everyone loved her. It's what made her feel worth something. *And I'm about to rock the family boat and dump everyone right into the water.*

But Tennie couldn't put her soul back to sleep. Scared as she was to speak up, the thought of sinking back to the bottom of her own heart hurt more. *Be brave, Tennessee,* she told herself. Fox could be right. Maybe people needed their pain.

And maybe they needed Tennie—just as she was—too.

"I, um . . ." Tennie tugged off her gloves. "I'd like to tell y'all why I wear my gloves. Or show you. If, um . . . Can somebody run grab me Poppy's walking stick from by the door?"

Shiloh brought it, and Tennie wrapped her shaking fingers around it. "Take my hand, Shi." Shiloh put her hand in Tennie's. As Poppy's gentle humming filled Tennie's head, Shiloh's eyes widened. Shi grabbed Birch's hand, and he blurted, "That's Poppy!"

The room went wild after that, and Lancaster grabbed hands with Lancaster until their tangle of crossed arms looked like the world's most disorganized prayer circle.

"Lord a'mercy, it's Harold," Mimsy gasped, then began to weep. "How're you makin' that happen?"

"I can pull secrets out of things with my fingers," Tennie said, staring at the floor. "Old secrets. Memories. I've been doing it for a long time, and even though I don't want to know things that ain't my business—" Her voice choked.

Everyone stared, speechless.

"I know a lot about all y'all. By accident, mostly. And . . . what I know worries me. A lot. I've been trying to fix everything for everyone all by myself. But I can't do that anymore." A flood of tears rushed out, and Tennie melted into her mom's and dad's arms.

Soon the whole thing came rushing out in a flood—the gloves, the memories, the secrets she never meant to find out. And the responsibility Tennie felt to use her superburden to make their lives easier.

"Let me get this straight," Dad said after he and Tennie stepped out to the porch for some air. "You've been keeping a piece of your tiara from your eighth birthday party—the party with the spiders and the barfing and the guests you missed out on—and using your memory-power-thing to punish yourself for bein' mad about it?"

"Well, not *punish*," Tennie said. "Just remind me to keep the peace. Everyone always has so many hard things going on. Mama was blue. She and Mimsy were fightin'. I just wanted to help."

"Tennie-Bean, you realize it's not your *fault* your mama

got depressed after the twins, right? It wasn't Mama's fault, either. It's just a chemical thing that happens sometimes. Being a paramedic is stressful. So was nursing twins."

"But . . . when I started helping out, she got better," Tennie pointed out, tucking her hair behind her ear nervously.

"And helpin' out is always appreciated. But your mama got better mostly 'cause she found a medication that gave her some chemicals her brain couldn't make. And she started talking to a counselor through her work."

Tennie's head snapped to the side. "She did?"

Dad squeezed her shoulder. "She sure did. Because she loves you more than anything."

Tennie frowned. "Then why didn't she talk about it?"

Dad was quiet for a long minute. "Seems like we all could do with more talking."

A few hours later, Tennie settled at the kitchen table, steaming cocoa in hand. Mimsy wrapped her long fingers around her bone china cup, and Mama gripped her coffee mug.

"I'm really new at this," Tennie said, jittery. "I know a lot of secrets, and if I step into anyone's business, I'm really sorry. But I've got some things to say."

"Alright, Storybook."

"Shoot, kiddo."

Tennie took a deep breath. "Y'all fight a lot. And I know it ain't 'cause you hate each other—I *know* that. But it really stresses me."

Mama sucked in a long breath, and Mimsy's bottom lip wobbled.

"Well, I've been thinking about this for a while. And since Tennie's being so brave, I think it's only fair I try and be brave, too," Mama said slowly. "Mom, it upsets me to hear you run Dad down about how much time he spent alone, especially now he's gone."

Mimsy sighed. "Darlin', you know I loved your daddy . . ."

Mama held up a finger. "It hurts because Dad and I were really similar. And I'm afraid to tell you I get depressed some-times, too. 'Cause I'm afraid of what you'll say about it. I'm worried you'll think I need to buck up, or that I'm not good enough. It's why I didn't call for a while, after the twins."

Mimsy's eyes brimmed with tears. "Well, I'm so glad you told me. I *missed* you." Mimsy sighed and frowned. "I can see how that might make you feel that way. Your daddy got so dis-tant sometimes, like he always had some secret worry. I never could convince him to let me cheer him up . . ." Mimsy blew her nose. "I reckon I felt useless, like a burden."

"I think I can help explain about Poppy, if you want," Tennie said softly, as Dad wandered in and kissed the top of her head.

Tennie told them about the hauntings, and about what Poppy's ghost had shown her about his hometown in Virginia. She told them what he said about trying to save the mountain by owning it, and always feeling guilty for failing his old home.

Mama, Dad, and Mimsy all came clean to one another about their money troubles, their apartment problems, and Mama's new pregnancy. The next several hours were full of pots of coffee, calculators, and a lot of honesty around Mimsy's breakfast table.

Mimsy wrung her hands. "We may have to sell the place. Not to Mr. Bolton, mind. But I can't see another way around it."

"But someone else'll come along and ruin the forest," Tennie half shouted, eyes threatening to spill. "There has to be another way besides all this stupid buyin' and sellin' and money!"

Finally, Dad scraped a hand over his whiskers. "You know, one of my friends worked on a project up in Wisconsin, where someone donated private property as a protected nature preserve. The community funds it, everyone together, and the original owner works as a custodian. Then, everyone enjoys it and makes sure it's given respect."

"Like a national park?" Tennie asked, brightening.

"Like a *Howler's Hollow* park. And it just so happens—" Dad cracked his knuckles and raised his eyebrows "—that y'all have a passionate community organizer and website designer in the family with a lot of free time on his hands."

"I love this idea," Mimsy said decidedly. "It sounds like work, but I'd hate for the land to fall into the hands of someone else like Russell after I'm gone. Me and the Rook Night ladies will spread the word and rally the troops. In the meantime, I think it's time we sold off some of Poppy's paintings. That should keep me afloat for now."

Tennie's heart ached with the hope of it all. "Could we dedicate the park in honor of the girls lost in that mudslide?" she suggested.

"That's a real nice idea, baby," Mama said, kissing her head.

"Alright, then. It's time for business. I'll need lots of hands to help me get the idea up and running," Mimsy said, clasping her hands together. "So, I'd like to ask you to all come live with me. As a favor, at least for a little while. We could all work together to keep the lights on."

Dad shot Mama a look, and Tennie held her breath. Mama reached over and grabbed Mimsy's hand, like they were going to arm wrestle. She gave it a tight squeeze. "Okay, Mama. For a little while."

Then, just like that, the world didn't fall apart. Love, like sadness, had its own gravity, and all the Lancasters pulled closer together, each in their own way.

After they'd put on a pot of beans for lunch and demolished every last crumb of Tennie's homemade birthday cake, they surprised Tennie with her own cell phone—compliments of her parents, Mimsy, and Birch combined. And when the sun sank deep into the cracks of the mountains, all of them headed down to the festival for Halloween night.

Heart spinning, Tennie drank in the smell of funnel cake, bought her sisters candied apples, and talked Birch into dancing with her as the Hollerin' Howlers—the local string band—played a fast, staccato cover of "This is Halloween."

Fox turned up bedecked in black feathers, glitter, and dark eyeliner—a human version of French Fry. As for Tennie's costume, tonight she was most happy to be her honest self. She couldn't have felt happier as anything else.

After being introduced to some kids from the Hollow—including a chatty friend of Tyler's and his serious-looking cousin—Fox and Tennie walked the corn maze together, hand in hand.

Sitting atop the platform in its center, Tennie rested her head on Fox's shoulder. Fox sighed and swung their legs happily.

It was the perfect thirteenth birthday.

Tennie never heard from Poppy's ghost or the marble ghosts again. And that was perfect, too. They'd told their story. Now, Tennie needed space to write her own.

Epilogue

One sticky afternoon during summer break, after a long spring semester at Howler Middle, Tennie and Fox sorted through tacky boxes of jewelry for Mimsy's shop. The idea was to pool their earnings and buy a canoe to go exploring the island in the middle of the lake at the north end of the Hollow—a plan Tennie was beginning to regret. She hated the heat.

Fox stuck their curly head out from around a tower of boxes in Mimsy's storage unit, face drawn and serious. "Hey, Tennie?"

"Hmmm?" Tennie asked, tossing a brooch with a missing rhinestone into the "junk" pile.

"Did you really *enjoy* ghost hunting?"

"Which part?" Tennie asked, tilting her head.

Fox bit their lip. "Any of it, I guess. Was it fun? Or did you just do it because you thought I wanted to?"

Tennie smiled wryly. *"Yes."*

"But the fun—what was it, scale of one to ten?"

"Eight and a half. I'd do it again, probably."

"Then I have a present for you."

Tennie held out a gloved hand. Fox dropped a rusty harmonica into her palm.

It was cold as ice.

Fox grinned and leaned closer, teasingly pulling the harmonica back. "You can still tap out, if you'd rather be bored. Last chance."

Tennessee Lancaster pursed her lips. "Oh, I think I can manage a touch of ruckus every now and then. Hand it here."

Acknowledgments

To my agent, Lauren Spieller: Thank you so much for being a fierce champion of my work. You really are a Valkyrie. This book exists partly due to your tenacity, and its title is perfect. Thanks also to the entire team at Triada US Literary.

To my editor, Jenne Abramowitz: Thank you for seeing this story's soul so clearly and for helping it be its best. It was a wild year, and I'm so grateful to have worked alongside someone as kind, talented, and passionate as you.

To every person at Scholastic whose skill and heart helped make these characters a reality, and to designer Baily Crawford and artist Steffi Walthall for lending their amazing talent to the cover.

To the friends and family: 2020 was a spectacularly difficult year, and somehow you found the time and energy to read and cheer me on in making this book happen. I hope I've done as good a job letting you know how very cherished you are. You rock my world.

Special thanks to Daniel and Justin for letting me borrow the gorgeous silence of your spare room while coffee houses weren't available. To Brody-dog-harbor-seal, for keeping my feet warm while I was there. Rest in rainbows, buddy; you'll always claim a fond corner of my heart.

To Juliana Brandt, Kit Rosewater, Brian Kennedy, and Erica Waters, for being amazing humans and for your feedback on this project during such a wild year. May your words always flow, you gorgeous folk. Thanks also to Laura Weymouth, for your feedback while helping jump-start my brain during Tennie's reboot in Austin.

N, thanks for adventuring with me, and putting up with my ghosts.

To the Otter-squad: your hugs, arguments, patience, generosity, humor, and fierceness make me a better human. I love you ten million, exactly the way you are. You're the fire in my bones.

About the Author

Ash Van Otterloo is the author of *Cattywampus*, an Indies Introduce and Indie Next pick. When they're not writing or freelance editing, they love gardening, hiking, exchanging playful banter, and collecting folklore stories. A former resident of the Smoky Mountains, they now live in Bremerton, Washington, with their spouse and four beautifully incorrigible children.